THE
PUNCH
BOOK
OF
SHORT
STORIES 3

THE PUNCH BOOK OF SHORT STORIES 3

Selected by *Alan Coren*

 Robson Books

FIRST PUBLISHED IN GREAT BRITAIN IN 1981 IN
ASSOCIATION WITH PUNCH PUBLICATIONS LTD.
BY ROBSON BOOKS LTD., 28 POLAND STREET,
LONDON W1V 3DB. THIS COLLECTION COPY-
RIGHT© 1981 ROBSON BOOKS.

The stories in this volume are reprinted by permission of
their authors whose copyright they remain.

British Library Cataloguing in Publication Data

Punch short stories. −3
  1. Short stories, English, Periodicals
  823'.01'08FS   PR1309.S5

  ISBN 0-86051-136-7

**Printed and bound in Great Britain
by Billing and Sons Limited
Guildford, London, Oxford, Worcester**

CONTENTS

DANIEL SIRICO

After a Few Years

Normally, I don't take the route through Beechwood. I have been taking the road that by-passes it every Wednesday for nearly six years now, but I don't go through it. This is not simply because of the by-pass; there are other small towns on my normal Wednesday route, just as there are other, different, small towns on my other routes, on other days, and I frequently come off the trunk roads for them. I stop for coffees I leave half-finished in the cup, I stop for cigarettes when I already have two packs in the glove compartment, sometimes I pull in for gas when the tank is three-quarters full. Occasionally, I just park at a meter, and walk around for a while, look in windows, check out house prices, ask a cop for directions to streets I already know. Sometimes I try on shoes, or try to find out if they can repair a calculator while I wait, and if they say yes, sure, then I tell them I'm going to collect it from the car, and I make a note not to go in the shop again.

I'm not too sure why I do all of this. It isn't as simple as bore-dom, if it were just boredom I'd go into bars; it certainly isn't curiosity, I have very little curiosity about anything. Some of it's about lying, I know that: I like to construct an elaborate lie about why the tank will only take three gallons, about why it is dangerous for me to drink an entire cup of coffee. When I do that, my skin moves. It's best when I put on a fake accent, South African, perhaps, or a muffed German consonant: I am a foreigner in a

strange town, a little lost, I need shoes, a flashlight battery. People
are nice to me.

Once or twice I have asked a cop directions and then deliberately walked in the opposite direction, feeling myself shaking,
waiting for him to come after me, redirect me, perhaps more
slowly, if it's one of my foreign days. On one occasion, I went
into an out-patient department and told the girl behind the
admissions desk that I was a registered addict, but I was a long
way from home, the other side of the country, and could they
please help me, and when she told me to take a seat I waited for
her to leave her desk and go through one of the three white doors
behind her, and then I left, running after I got out of the door,
and driving like hell until I got back on the by-pass.

Well, it breaks up the day. It breaks up life, introducing possi-
bilities, danger, alternatives. After a few years, you need that kind
of thing; you need to flirt with alternatives, since it is too late to
adopt them. I could, after all, have *been* a foreigner, all I had to do
was go somewhere else, I could have been a junkie, I could have
been the sort of person who gets through calculators at a remarkable rate. Had I chosen, twenty years ago, to slit my mother's
throat instead of going into sales management, for example, I
could now be getting ready to come out of jail, into an unknown
world, a new life, a person feared, probably, a person unfathomable, certainly, a person for whom every relationship would have
been totally different from those I currently enjoy, or do not enjoy,
by simple virtue of the fact that, in one brief second, I had
snatched up a cut-throat razor and. But I would have been the
same person, at root, that I am now. Isn't that odd? After all, the
decision to go into sales management took far longer, involved
far more, than cutting a throat on impulse.

I have made a lot of deliberated decisions like that, and hated
pretty well all of them. Hated the *process* of making them. You
could say that that was the reason I avoided Beechwood for so
many years, when it would have been so easy to take a conscious
decision to turn off the highway, make a left at the Presbyterian

church, take the second right off Walnut Street. I have the whole
plan of the place laid out in my head, I have studied large-scale
maps of the town, it is as familiar to me as my own. But I did not
want to plan to go there.

I did not tell the whole truth earlier. I am quite sure why I
spend so much time screwing around in all the other little towns.
It is to avoid going to Beechwood. They take the heat out of my
anguish at refusing to make a conscious decision to go to Beechwood. I get excited, driving the trunk roads, knowing that I am
answerable to no one in my present position and can go anywhere
I damn well choose during the course of my professional day;
can therefore go to Beechwood anytime I decide to, and see her.

I just decided not to decide to, is all.

But I was forty yesterday, and this morning I took the route
through Beechwood.

It was not a decided decision: my heart clanged in my throat,
and I made the exit.

Why should forty do it? A liver-spot on the hand, an ache in a
crown (they have to be replaced regularly, after forty), a vein on
my instep that displays a varicose cordedness, low back pain when
I swung my legs out of bed gingerly on a birthday morning,
when once I might have sprung? The sense that life has two
pivots, one at half forty, one at half death?

Anyway.

I had expected my blood to race rather more, I had expected to
become dizzy, as I passed the Presbyterian church, but I did not,
it felt quite normal, it felt as if, say, I were going to Redwing or
Danville to ask an undertaker if they could quote me for burying
my child or a chemist if he could suggest a bath-oil for someone
with eczema. Beechwood is a little town just like those, grass
verges, few cars over three years old, middle-aged men raising
their hats to women, white laundry vans, no buildings much over
ten storeys, plane trees, blacks hardly in evidence, a small park, a
library with glass walls.

I took the second right off Walnut Street, drove past her house quickly, noted the navy blue door, assessed its rough market value. Her husband had not done particularly well. I drove to the end of the street, made the block, came past her house again, more slowly, drove again to the end of the street, stopped. I felt sick, lit a cigarette, coughed, brought up a little pale bile, folded it into a Kleenex.

There was a call-box across the street.

'Sarah?'

'Who is this?'

'Has my voice changed that much?'

'My God.'

'I had to come to Beechwood. There was a, that's to say, my company is thinking of opening up here. Expansion, all that, times are very good if you have nerve, don't let anyone tell you different.'

'My God. Well, *my God*!'

'I only have an hour or so, could we meet, have a drink, coffee, that kind of thing?'

'I . . . what do you think?'

'What do I *think*? After a few years, I think it would be nice to have a cup of coffee.'

'Do you have my address?'

'It's in the phone book. They usually are.'

'Of course. I didn't, well, *my God*!'

'Five minutes?'

I redrove the road slowly, as if searching for the house, parked outside, walked briskly towards the door, like someone just dropping in for coffee on a chill day. There was a blue Datsun in the drive with a broken tail-light, but I did not take this as evidence that her husband was home, since this was not a street inhabited by men who drive damaged compacts.

'Don't say *my God* again,' I said. I could see past her, indeed was *looking* past her, at the paper in the hall, a faint apple-green stripe, one of ours, middle of the range, but not cheap, if perhaps vulgar in its very unostentatiousness.

'What should I say, then?'

'You should say: *If I should meet thee after long years, how should I greet thee? With silence and tears*, and I should reply: Jesus Christ, *Shelley!* I haven't read Shelley in—what is it?—twenty years, I haven't read Shelley since you and I used to read it together in college, for God's sake! That,' I said, smiling one of the smiles that has made me not only popular but commercially, I think, successful, 'is what you should say and what I should reply, but it's a hell of a lot to get through standing on the mat, on a cold day, so why don't you just say *my God* again?'

'You handle mat talk pretty well,' she said.

'I had a lot of practice.'

We went inside. The hallway smelt of recently aerosoled violets.

'But then you got successful.'

'But then I got successful,' I said. 'Now I control the decor of half a state.'

She led me into a split-level parlour, old Sahara paintwork, Navaho Sunset walls, reproduction Colonial furniture with all the software in colour-co-ordinated browns, the curtains in one of our cheaper golds, but faked with double-linings. They probably ran short of money when they got to the curtains, a lot of people do.

'I didn't even know you knew my married name,' she said, 'let alone where I live.'

'I keep tabs on all, well, kinds of people. Then there's my memory. I even took a course in it.'

'There's an ashtray somewhere,' she said. 'We don't smoke.'

'Don't we?'

'What?'

'I'm sorry. It slipped out. Other relationships, other con-spiracies. We say we at home a lot, too, it gets automatic. I'll use this saucer, I can tell it isn't much, it has earth in it, I'll use it till your plant gets back, it won't mind. They can take more punish-ment than people realise, plants. All that stuff about talking to them, that's just, well, crazy people. Lonely people, I mean.' I put

the cigarette out. 'They made us read whole pages of the encyclo-
paedia.'

'Who did?'

'On this memory course I did. I got to be able to read a whole
page and memorise it in under three minutes. I still know more
about lepidoptera and charged particles than practically anybody
in the world. How about that?'

'You look thin.'

'I rush about a lot.'

'I'm sorry. It was a silly thing to say after twenty years.'

'What isn't?'

'Do you have children?'

'No, I don't. You have three, right? Cora and Joseph and little
Alison.'

'Dear God!'

I tapped my forehead.

'All up here with *argynnis paphia*, largest of the fritillaries,' I
said, and laughed, and she laughed, too. There was a dull small
thud from beyond the room.

'Percolator,' she said. 'It does it.'

'They do.'

'I'd have it fixed,' she said, 'only there's nothing wrong with the
coffee it makes, so let it, you know, thunk.'

'Remember that percolator we had at 1197 Chestnut with
perfect pitch?' I said. 'Didn't it used to resonate with Kid Ory
solos?'

'You must tell me about your work,' she said, after a few
seconds.

'Yes', I said. 'It's wonderful. If you'd stayed with me, you'd
have got to see many of America's finest furnishing fabrics months
before they even reached the shops. You see how unexpected life
can be?'

She smiled. The percolator grunted. In the room, I could smell
the long presence of her children. I know what these fabrics smell
like when they come fresh off the mills.

'I'll get the coffee.'

When she was no longer there, I called:

'You're still very beautiful.'

She called:

'Cream and sugar?'

'This is a nice design,' I said, a little later. I turned the saucer over.

'We bought them in Germany. We try to get across to Europe every three or four years. I mean, not just to buy things, of course.'

'No, no,' I said, 'I realise that.'

'Do you go at all?'

'We went on our honeymoon. We hired a VW and went all over. I had a bad time in Venice.' I waited, but her eyes were neutral. 'Do you remember how you and I planned to live in Venice? Why did we pick on Venice, for God's sake?'

'I pass. I don't have your memory.' She did that funny old thing with her eyebrow. 'What I know about butterflies you could put on a pin. But then again—are you all right?'

I put the cup down on a little fake side table, just in time.

'Sorry. An involuntary tremor. Someone walked over my life. These carpets don't stain, they're impregnated. I still love you, Sarah, there hasn't been an hour in twenty years when I didn't know that.'

'Please.'

'It's all right, I have no plans to embarrass either of us,' I said. 'It isn't a statement I want to elaborate on, and there isn't anything else I want to talk about, the only plans I ever made about coming here and saying it were those in which I determined never ever to come here and say it; up until now my best decisions were always my negative ones.' I got up, and my knee hit the fake table, but it did not fall. 'As a matter of fact, my real plan for this afternoon was to be in East Camden speaking to an oculist in broken French, or possibly getting a quote from a caterer for a really big party I shan't be throwing, that just shows you how much of an accident my being here is, doesn't it?'

'Please don't rush off like this.'

'You don't really mean that.'

'I don't really know what I mean.'

'What I'm afraid of is staying long enough to ask whether you ever loved me, back when. After a few years . . .'

'Twenty.'

I opened the door.

'Sleet,' I said. It was coming out of the slate sky, slanting. 'I ought to be going anyhow. When it's icy, my husband worries.'

MELVYN BRAGG

Indian Love Calls

1 Sounding

'And here is another erotic,' the guide said, looking expectantly at me for an appropriate response. I gazed up to the face of the ancient Temple of Love. 'There,' he insisted, his abrupt English peppering the air with faint showers of spittle. 'Above the elephant with the legs of a lion full of imagination.' He pointed fiercely. Taking my time, I picked my way through the maze of intricate stonework until I came across the happy couple. This time the woman straddled the man, clinging around him like a child while he, quite clearly seen from below, penetrated her. Nine hundred years, I thought, without moving.

It was all becoming too much to absorb. Like a drowned body which has taken in its fill of water so that it can be bloated no further, I was already filled full after my first few days in India. And the heat; June—the worst month, everyone had said so.

But the Temple was magnificent—and the afternoon was my only time free. 'Another!' rapped out my guide, imperiously. A self-appointed guide. My new friend, Dr Mitra, had gone back to the car to bring a book. 'There,' said the guide, this time, I thought, daring me to be expressionless. Once again I searched among the rows of elephants, the smiling dancing girls, the kings and beasts and warriors to find one of the famous 'erotics'. There it was. The guide noted that I had settled on it. 'You see,' he explained, where very little explanation was necessary, 'the man is kneeling on the ground and with his tongue he is enticing the genitals of the lady to sexually excite her. In the meantime his friend is standing beside the lady and admiring her structures. "Oh," he is saying, "how beautiful you are." His hand, you will observe, is on her mammary gland.'

Gently, Dr Mitra unclipped me from the single-minded guide and we continued the tour in a rather more general way. But there was no escaping the 'erotics'. Nor did I particularly want to.

Interpreting my silence from heat, Dr Mitra led the way to the shade of a large banyan tree. He went to get some fresh coconut milk while I gazed up at the magical Temple built like a chariot with twenty-seven wheels and seven galloping horses drawing it towards the morning sun which rose from the ocean a few score yards away. It was both monumental and exquisite and most of all, perhaps like every great work of art, it was serene. Even the 'erotics' were displayed and placed without shame or furtive fidgeting. The peace, the wholeness, all that India promised, seemed fulfilled here.

My own disaffection seemed no more than an irrelevant itch on this huge body of achieved tranquillity. It seemed so trivial, a western worry about love and fidelity. Yet it would not go away. And I had promised myself I would resolve it and go back home with a fixed course of action.

It was not only the sensual completeness of this Temple, but also what I had seen and learned of Indian marriage which diminished the significance of my 'problem'. These arranged marriages, which had seemed so absurd, from a distance of six thousand miles, now appeared so sensible and so civilised; above all so stable. Dr Mitra, a scholar and something of a poet, had spent the previous evening talking about such marriages, expressing his concern about 'finding wives' for his brothers, spelling out the costs and complications of the system—the horoscopes, the rituals, the ceremony. But what came through most beguilingly was a sense of calm. Marriage was recognised as a profound public institution which needed the most powerful rules to protect it. But within the rules was, it seemed, some tranquillity.

Such arrangements, far from being absurd, now appeared to be the wisest way to ensure that constancy of family life. And the 'erotics' fall into place as the natural counter-point of that chaste wisdom.

Dr Mitra had still not returned and perhaps the heat and the fatigue from so much travel and so much newness was weakening any critical judgement I might have had. The institution and the open sensuality—our western freedom of love palled a little in comparison with these intertwined pillars. The Temple, in full sunlight, glowered with that interplay. All we could hold against it, perhaps, was the *force* of freely given affection. How strong was mine?

The coconut milk was warm. After drinking it, I continued to pretend to be a little tired: too many turbulent questions beat off that serene Temple. We went down to the beach—to miles of empty sands, speckled by one or two fishing villages humped in the dunes as naturally as the dunes themselves. The whole day, the whole trip now began to merge in this slowly revolving kaleidoscope of different ways of loving. Which was better? Which mattered? The questions heaved up as slowly as the dunes heaved back from the sea which roared along the length of the shore.

A few boys heeled the sand for crabs. One or two youths slung out a line. Nearly naked, they ignored us totally as we sat on the sand and talked a little of literature and the history of his state— Orissa—Dr Mitra's two preoccupations. A few yards away the pre-biblical split boats of the fishermen were receiving some attention ready for the morning when they would sweep out twenty kilometres to the sea and sometimes stay there for days until they had a catch worth bringing in. Seven days a week they fished. This work was their entire life. God alone knew the deprivation and hardships, but for me once again it was the serenity which came through: and again it questioned one's own activity.

It seemed to be a day which drew everything to one end—for,

during one of our long, amiable silences, I noticed that the boys
digging for bait did not speak to each other at all. They were
lively; they were as rapid as little lizards in their movements, but
they said nothing. As the thought came to my mind, Dr Mitra
smiled at me and said, 'They do not need to talk. Sometimes it is
better not to say anything.' I nodded and smiled a little as if to
allay the strangeness of such empathy.

Yet as we walked back to the Temple to see it once again, this
time under the floodlights, I could not let go the nag of decision
which gnawed at the ankles of my mind and would not be shaken
off. Somehow, on this day, at this time, in a place devoted to the
idea and the fact which so preoccupied me, I could take a decision,
make a change, trust in the thought.

The peace of the Temple under the floodlights was palpable.
Young boys walked softly around the boundary walls together,
hand in hand. The great chariot seemed to roll under the lights
and the granite gods glittered back at the unnatural illumination.

Dr Mitra led me to the north side where we looked through the
two heraldic beasts and, although it was hard to believe because
it was so ridiculously appropriate, listened to a flute being played,
gently, expertly, somewhere in the forest behind us.

So, I thought, think the thoughts; take the decision; do it.
And like an adolescent at a confirmation I wished for what I
wanted. When I opened my eyes I was looking at one of the life-
size dancing girls which decorated the top of the Temple.

'They are telling us of our past,' said Dr Mitra, dark in the
darkness beside me. 'They are bringing us messages from our
past.' And was my message travelling even now? I would know,
on my return: I would ask.

'They say,' Dr Mitra continued, after a while, 'that at night,
late, late at night, the dancing girls come alive. They dance for
us.' Yet again his tone was light, exactly poised, ambiguous—
believe me or believe me not, it said.

I looked again and even then noticed one of the 'erotics' and
remembered the excited guide. I had thought of them enstoned,

like Keats's figures on a Grecian Urn, never moving.

It was as if the heat of the day lifted and with it lifted the stealthy perturbation of such thoughts and impressions as it had brought on.

And the 'erotics', I wanted to ask, did *they* move? Late, late at night, did they move? I hoped so.

As if he had heard my unspoken question Dr Mitra laughed, gently, even merrily. 'We can go now,' he said.

A white eagle swept in from the forest, lifted to the top of the monument, banked, pivoted and swooped back into the darkness. We stopped and watched it, silently. I had never seen one before.

2 *The Last Post*

'I'm told you're available for a wee interview.' The Scottish accent was so pure it could have been a hoax. But an expert Glaswegian mimic seemed unlikely in circumspect New Delhi. I realised I had allowed a discourteous pause to develop and promptly ended it with as weak an assent as I could politely deliver. All I wanted was an evening alone. 'It won't be too long or too painful, laddie,' he assured me, a small laugh in the voice. I liked his quickness and agreed to meet him in the hotel bar in half an hour.

Was it a dry day? Was some unfathomable festival being celebrated which insisted that alcohol be banned? I needed a drink and I was annoyed that I had not been sufficiently alert to ask him to my room: the management prided itself on its sophistication: tourists were, rather pityingly I thought, served alcohol in their bedrooms twenty-four hours a day.

But the bar was not dry. I ought to have trusted him. I soon learned to.

Jim Lithgow was irresistible. Having clawed his way up from

the back streets of Glasgow, so the tale ran, he was now somewhere adrift in his fifties. He had come to India more than twenty
years ago and stayed on. He had exactly that rueful, philosophic-
ally creased face which seems to speak of private defeats stoically
borne. His undiluted Scottishness was like a cold breeze across
the oceanic warmths of the ever yielding sub-continent. Even his
shabby clothes smacked, somehow, of an independent spirit.

'I'm supposed to be interviewing you, laddie,' he said after an
hour or so spent gossiping. 'Give me some relevant facts—not too
many—and a couple of intelligent remarks about, what is it you
are peddling?—Contemporary British Literature—that'll do—
and we'll round it off with some duly respectful observations on
India. Heads down.'

He took the few notes in shorthand in one of those small note-
books supplied free in the bedrooms of the better hotels. He
noticed my glance. 'Do you have any in your room?' he asked.
'They're far 'n' away the handiest things I've come across.'

His smile was almost wolfish, such pleasure it devoured from
the notion of these small token notepads being available for his
work.

He had come to India as a foreign correspondent but he was
disinclined to talk about that: nor was he forthcoming on the way
in which he cobbled together his present livelihood. But on
almost everything else—it seemed to me—matters Indian, British,
Russian, American, military, political, private, scandalous and
sometimes serious, he gossiped with the greatest relish imaginable.

At one stage he must have made a study (although that phrase
would never cross his mind let alone his lips) of the various Indian
myths and he led me through those incredible entanglements as
lightly as a will-o'-the-wisp. And there was something light,
flitting, ungraspable about him for all his Celtic clarity. He chose
the most audacious of the stories, tales of fantastical love and
demented passion, relishing their baroque details. Yet there was
no scorn in him: he gave the stories their due.

'But you didn't come here to learn about India, laddie,' he said sharply, pulling himself up short. 'Now did you?'

There was no answer to that.

He had the quality of putting you, visibly, in a corner. I was reluctant to leave him and surprised to find how muzzy my head was. We had drunk rather a lot. I paid. He walked off, brisk as a sea captain.

I had come to India to do some research on Anglo-Indian literature and the next days were swallowed up in work. I found that I kept thinking about him, wondering why such an uneventful, chatty couple of hours should have left such a mark.

His name came up at a buffet lunch in the house of the Acting Head of the British High Commission. In that elegant 'bungalow', almost but not quite replicating Surrey crossed with Harrods, where the fluted English sentences rose high under the whirling fans and the brightly turbaned bearers brought in drinks from long ago, the man who had been justifying the policies of Mrs Indira Gandhi said, 'Lithgow rattled her with that piece of his in the Emergency. I'm told she'll never forgive him. Not that he needs any more bad luck, poor sod. But he was still up to it, even as recently as that.'

It was only after the lunch and from a junior member of the Commission that I learned more.

Lithgow had fallen 'absurdly' (that was the word, delivered on the back of a laugh like a letter on a salver) in love with an Indian widow of 'no particular distinction that anyone could make out'. He had married her, western style, and then tried to bring her into that decorous diplomatic, journalistic and political quadrille which represented Delhi society. There was no reason why he should not have succeeded. Odder things had happened. It was considered rather foolhardy for him to quit his job with the paper but, as he said, London could no longer afford a full-time man in India and he could no longer afford to be full-time in London. He would freelance. Everyone knew he had stayed for his wife's sake and his stock rose, if anything. But he had always been well liked and admired.

The change came rather swiftly. His wife had soon ceased to come to any of the parties. She had nothing to say to anyone and was most often to be found outside the door standing or squatting, glance averted, sari half-drawn over her face, waiting to be gone. He had taken the dangerous step from heavy to dependent drinker. There were stories that she had gone back to her parents, to her village. He disappeared for several months and returned to find his two most important contacts gone. Soon after that he moved into Old Delhi. No one knew now whether he lived with his wife or not. He appeared to have contained the drinking but there was an edge to him, an unreliability which had been much more damaging to his career and reputation than either the Hindu wife or the alcohol.

The young man was reluctant to spell out what this was. Perhaps he did not quite know. More likely he thought he had blurted out quite enough. The most I could learn was that Lithgow had become 'rather crazy about this woman' and 'a bit too pro-Indian'.

It might have ended there. I was intrigued but there was no reason for me to pursue it. Nor would I have done but I saw him, a couple of evenings later, in a small eating-house in the warrens of Old Delhi.

It was my last night and I was restless to see more of the 'real' place, as I could not help describing it, even though the fear of seeming to patronise would have frozen the word on my tongue. There was a censor chopping out every second thought.

I had taken a taxi which rattled down the middle of the ambassadorial avenues of the New Town and suddenly came across the jungle-jumble of Old Delhi. The air was heavy, damply hot; the monsoon was being promised and prayed for but as yet it was no more than a tease—a little shower here and there, a flirt.

Old Delhi with its esplanades of crumbling grandeur, its garland of single naked electric light bulbs dangling above all manner of food and trinkets, its rickshaw-wallahs, beggars, back-alleys, temples, street-cries and flux of people and traffic, appeared like an Asian cliché. People seethed up the streets—children beggar-dressed mixed with tiny tots turned out as if for a wedding. Displays, toys, clothes, jewels, and stores of all kinds were laid out on the ground or piled on stalls—always arranged with precision and artistry. The smells were rich. The mood was gentle, and yet, I had been told to watch out; white Europeans could become targets.

The side streets were too picturesquely tempting to be resisted. Yet again there was that tug: picturesque? Poor, rather, and deprived. But on this last night nothing could deprive the Englishman of his wallow in the labyrinths of the Old Town.

Jim waved me in though I noticed a momentary reluctance and felt a corresponding hesitation. If he had his reasons for being alone, then so had I. But the pressure of politeness was too much even for what might have been quite deep contrary impulses. I went in and sat down beside him. I had eaten. While he finished his meal—or rather while he played with it; his appetite for solids was not great—I had a beer.

He looked shabbier, even seedy, and his face showed signs of the approach of saturation point—reddening nose, heavy flush on the cheeks, eyes sometimes fumbling for focus.

'So what message will you take back to the British, laddie?' he asked after I'd explained that it was my last night.

'I've no idea. It's overwhelming.'

'Overwhelming.' He repeated the word and seemed to put it on a set of scales and weigh it up carefully. Then he nodded. 'That'll do,' he said.

A sudden awkwardness entered, palpably almost like an unwelcome intruder. I was about to manoeuvre myself away when he said: 'Let's go for a real drink.'

Outside, his mood become buoyant; clearly he adored the place and he zig-zagged through the narrow streets with assurance and pleasure. One of his delights was to point out the signs in English —'The Very Old Shop', one read, and another 'Universal Centre of Thought, Philosophy and Electronic Information: Entrance

Backside', 'TIP TOP Laundry Cleaners' and 'For best examination
of Blood, Urine, Sputum, Stools—queue here, thank you'. One
of his favourites was 'Southern Skin Centre' but best of all was a
sign which advertised calor gas; underneath was printed 'HIHELY
INFALAMABEL'. This was crossed out and in larger, much more
authoritative letters, the sign was amended to 'HIGHLIE INFAM-
MBLE'.

Yet his enjoyment was not patronising. When he caught me
glancing at the old men crossed-legged in a doorway, smoking or
more simply staring; or pausing to look up some passage off an
alley where there would be a scene so striking as to look like a
film set—an up-ended motorbike, say, being worked on by three
or four young men in gaudy shirts and jeans while elders and
children, cows and goats squatted and stumbled around them as
if in the remotest village: or merely registering too avidly,
perhaps, the vivacity of the street life—then I would sense a
growing disapproval. It was as if his protectiveness about India
and its people was so deep and so refined that the reactions of no
other Briton were tolerable.

We came to a place where he was well known, another small
bare room off a narrow side street, and a bottle of Bell's whisky
was produced by the manager. Three doubles were poured and
Jim paid before touching a drop.

He swallowed the first mouthful carefully, having measured in
a well-disciplined quantity of cold water.

'It never lets you down,' he said, and grinned like a schoolboy.

The scotch erased any uneasiness and soon we were chatting
as freely as at our first meeting. The bottle of Bell's came and
went. Jim's reserve or his reservations left him and he ranged over
the Raj, Kipling, the possible effect of Sanjay Gandhi's recent
death on Indian politics—and then he settled on the dowry system
and spoke of the way in which girls of five were married off in
some of the more backward provinces, of how prostitution was
organised, of the darker side of that pacific face of the arranged
marriage which had struck me as being so surprisingly sensible

and successful. As he spoke, my curiosity about his life and his present circumstances grew—but it was impossible to ask him the sort of direct questions which would have given the answers I wanted.

I noticed her without recognising the fact at first. Just another lean, slight, young teenage girl in a doorway. One of the tens of thousands stopping to stand and stare. But she was in my eye-line —behind Jim—and her glance across to our table was unmistakably persistent. As he talked on, I felt the persistence of that glance and could not interpret it. She was no prostitute: nor was she a beggar: nor did she look the sort to gawp at two white men getting drunk—she looked too intelligent for that.

Jim caught my glance and looked around. He beckoned and the girl came over.

'My daughter,' he said.

She pressed her palms together and bowed. The look of matronly anxiety sat sadly on her young slim face.

'Time for home,' he told her. He turned to me. 'You've caught me on one of my jaunts. I don't play truant very often. Sometimes you have to.'

He said something in Hindi to the manager and the three of us went out.

'I'll take you to where you can pick up a taxi,' he said. 'It can get a wee bit worrying at this time of night.'

Perhaps his words prompted me to look for other things but I did notice a change as we went back towards the main thoroughfare. The crowd was not as yielding. The groups of young men called out in Hindi and then laughed at the jokes they had made at our expense. The beggars were less servile, the vendors more claimant. Jim watched my reaction to all of this. His daughter followed us, subdued, light on her feet, resigned. She was very beautiful. Chancing it, I said as much to Jim.

He was pleased.

'Her mother,' he said, by way of explanation.

Had he other children?

'Two more—younger. Shukla'—that was his daughter's name
—'brings them up.' We were in a quiet street, taking a short cut.
'Their mother died,' he said stolidly. 'Went back to her village
and decided to die.'

He was looking ahead of him as he said the words and neither
his pace nor his manner altered during their delivery. But the
wound was bared for anyone with eyes to see. The wound and the
terrible loss. I remembered the phrase about his being 'rather
crazy about this woman'.

We reached the main street. He saw me into a taxi.

We shook hands. His daughter bowed once more. The bone-
shaking taxi cut a swathe through the crowd as it turned to make
for New Delhi. My last sight of Jim Lithgow was of him walking
away back into the side streets, his shoulders braced in imitation
of his former briskness, his daughter at his shoulder like a
guardian.

3 An Arranged Marriage

It began soon after I arrived at the University for a three month
stint as a visiting lecturer.

Baschia was in the English Department. He was an elegant
young Brahmin who had completed his education in America.
The quality of his published work, on the contemporary American novel, would almost certainly have guaranteed him a post in
one of the better colleges there. But he had insisted on returning
to what he only half-ironically called 'my native soil'. He would
smile after using the phrase, look around at the desert landscape
which provided a barren carpet for most of this impoverished
Indian province and add: 'As you can see—soil is about all we
have to offer.' By such low-key self-mockeries he would deflect
any criticism of the place he clearly loved.

She was called Sushma and she had come to the University to
do her M.A. on the novels of Saul Bellow. Many of the young
women on the campus were lovely to look at—the sensuous
composure, the rather long oval faces set off by expressions lit up
with innocent merriness: Sushma was a beauty. Baschia fell for
her the moment he set eyes on her.

'It's quite interesting,' he would say, striving to minimise and
at the same time explain his blatant love-sickness. 'The phrase
"love at first sight"—so rich in meaning to both our cultures—
to all cultures quite possibly—is yet no more than a figure of
speech until it happens to oneself.' Yes, Baschia, we would say,
trying not to smile. He was so intoxicated that by his own
countrymen's standards, he was behaving most unbecomingly—
though with a honourable naiveté and charming formality. 'I am
sorry to bring up the subject of Sushma yet again,' he would say,
when he had been out of her sight for some intolerable time—say
a couple of hours, 'but Dr Mitra was saying the other day that he
thought she was a little too tall—not much—but just a little *too*
tall. What is your opinion?' And again we would give all our
attention to him because it was so nice and so rare to see such a
fine man so wonderfully in love with such a beauty.

They walked together from lecture to lecture. He would chop
up the pattern of his own studies and his own teaching to escort
her from the English Studies building to the Canteen or the
General Humanities faculty or the Hostel. He always had his
umbrella—to shade her from the sun or protect her from the rain.
It was just before the monsoons when the weather could alter
violently.

They were lovely to watch and soon they became part of our
daily conversation. 'I saw them this morning in the old town—
about 6 o'clock. I believe he was showing her the Tantric temple:
she looked very interested!' And we would nod happily at the
thought and gain a little extra pleasure from the picture of him
being the earnest teacher, she the solemn student. For they never
touched in public, they did not hold hands; they could indeed

have been mistaken by the uninitiated for teacher and student. 'I saw them in the lunch hour, in the blazing heat, over where they keep promising to build the Sports-drome—she was wearing one of those marvellous golden saris of hers: Baschia of course was looking like a peasant, as usual!' And yet again there would be complicity—for her wealthy parents endowed her with clothes fit indeed for her beauty and Baschia's principles decreed that, unlike all his colleagues, he should revert to traditional Indian peasant wear. In those few weeks, while he wooed her and won her in as courtly a way as could be imagined, they were like figures from a jewelled and precious miniature painting come to life as reminders of magic and fortune on this otherwise dull and bare plain in the middle of India.

'What will happen now?' I asked my friend Dr Mitra. 'Oh, his parents will approach her parents. They will have their horoscopes taken. The usual procedures.' Dr Mitra enjoyed guiding me through the infinite variety of Indian social codes. 'To all intents and purposes it will go ahead like all our arranged marriages. They have had the luck to fall in love and spend time getting to know each other.' That latter phrase sounded rather a tame description of the passion that clearly possessed Baschia, but I thought no more of it at the time. The extent and the apparent success of these arranged marriages still daunted me. From my English viewpoint, the system seemed to drive out all love and all liberty: yet, it worked so well, I was still, as it were, collecting evidence on that.

Unexpected and most unwelcome evidence came soon. Dr Mitra told me that Sushma had moved in with Baschia. He had the usual senior lecturer's flat on the outskirts of the campus. This 'shacking up together', so common in the West, was greeted with dismay and sadness by everyone in the University. People felt let down. More than that they truly mourned what they predicted as the end of any real chance of happiness for the young couple. And they felt that the place would suffer some slight dishonour.

Yet their behaviour was good. The jokes went and so did all the tender by-play of reference—but the couple were not ostracised nor were they publicly or privately rebuked. But people withdrew. Where before there had been a sense in which everyone was participating in this wonderful drama—there was now a distinct and rather ominous feeling of pulling back to a boundary, no longer being prepared to participate, watching the drama from the sidelines. To the observers, the outcome was very obvious.

Dr Mitra was reluctant to talk about it—the whole business upset him too much. Baschia was not only a particular friend but someone he had admired in a whole-hearted and loving way. Eventually I was told Sushma came from a lower caste. Her parents were very wealthy and they did not want her to be wasted on a poor university lecturer, Brahmin or not. As soon as he had learned of this, he had taken her to live with him.

To me they seemed just as happy, even happier now that they were, presumably, sleeping together. They still retained their own magic and walked through the place as if girded by an invisible and benevolent wall. Where others saw a couple doomed, I saw the irresistible unfolding of a rare love affair. I had never seen such a combination of courtesy, affection, and, I did not doubt it, sexual satisfaction.

Always true to himself, Baschia had made a brilliant move. About fifty miles from the University there was one of India's most famous and ancient Hindu Temples. In that place the priests had the power to marry. Before moving in together, Baschia and Sushma had gone to the Temple and been married in a ceremony older even than the rituals which attended an arranged marriage. They've managed it, I thought—the perfect combination—a real and free love affair and an ancient, traditional marriage. The idea of this gave me inordinate pleasure. It proved something for both East and West.

The end came very swiftly. I heard it from Dr Mitra who had been part of the drama.

Her parents had arrived. Rich, Dr Mitra explained, Indian merchant rich—professing themselves deeply hurt that their daughter was prepared to ignore her caste and their feelings in this way. It intrigued me that they were opposed to Baschia even though he was from a caste so superior to their own: in English class terms it would represent an advantageous match well worth a businessman's daughter and dowry. Not in India, Dr Mitra insisted: and besides—for he was not without worldliness—they wanted the connection with another wealthy family which a particularly beautiful daughter could bring them.

They had taken over a floor of the best local hotel and, with some difficulty, persuaded the young couple to come and see them. The Head of Police had been there, the Mayor, a most hang-dog Vice-Chancellor of the University, Sushma's two elder brothers who were 'Mafia types' and her three younger sisters who had burst into genuine and affecting tears at the sight of their disgraced sister. Dr Mitra had been there at Baschia's invitation.

The strategy, Dr Mitra explained, grimly, had been to try to separate them. Her father wept and roared; the Head of Police looked solemn and talked about the legality of Temple weddings and the danger to public morals of such permissive co-habitation; the Mayor had spoken up for family obedience; the Vice-Chancellor had wrung his hands. Baschia and Sushma had met every objection with serious and sound arguments.

Then her mother had been brought in melodramatically, with cynical manipulation in mind—and Sushma had agreed to go into another room above to talk to her. Baschia's resistance seemed churlish—a mother and her daugher must be allowed to talk privately together? He was overruled. He shook her hand, said Dr Mitra, his eyes misting a little, and gave a little bow. Then he sat down to wait. That was just after 10 p.m.

'We were still in the same room in the same position twelve hours later,' said Dr Mitra, a little shamefacedly. 'Every time Baschia tried to go through to see her, he was blocked by some of the police the Headman had brought along. One by one her family disappeared and we all knew what had happened. They had taken her away. They had kidnapped her.'

Over the next few weeks I saw Baschia every day and every day he seemed more tired, more ill, less and less himself. The message from her parents was that she was free to marry anyone but at the moment was making up her mind. The private information was that she had been locked in her room, was guarded night and day by servants and bodyguards, accompanied even to the bathroom and systematically beaten.

Baschia can do nothing. He has neither the money nor the legal basis to bring an action to retrieve her. He went to their house but was run out of the town by the local police who are in her parents' pockets. He knows his letters don't reach her. She has been unable to send a single message to him since that last formal handshake.

He knows she will never give in. His feeling for her weakens him daily. There are those, already, who say that he will die quite soon.

ALAN HACKNEY

Casting

In the restaurant the agent said: 'You Italians know nothing about your history. It's ridiculous, when it's all around you.'

'We are like that,' shrugged Franco, smiling co-operatively, and Valentina didn't say anything for the moment, trying instead to project an air of watchful intelligence, which was quite taxing enough. She sipped her espresso decorously.

The agent had already had his lunch, with the old count, which did no harm to his image. The actors had only been invited for coffee, which they understood. The agent was from Lebanon, probably, an Arab at any rate. As clients, lunch was when you were working and getting paid.

'You can stand in front of the Colosseo and ask someone where it is and they won't know,' said the agent, a young man with a restless eye. 'People are simply not alert. Well, for instance, do you know why the airport is called the Leonardo da Vinci?'

'No,' said Franco. Was an actor supposed to know everything?

'It's named after one of your famous aviators,' said the agent. 'There's a statue of him there. You pass it every time you go to the airport.'

Outside in the street, the Roman spring had shown up for three days now, and the daily flood of warm golden stage lighting was working its annual magic on the movie makers.

'Space pictures are out,' the agent affirmed. 'We all know that. History is in. Medieval is in. Porno is still in for the moment. In any case, Rossi is finally doing his Garibaldi, as a co-production. He is casting next week and I'm talking to him each day. I've told him you're both free.'

'Who did the script?' asked the old count.

'It is a very good script,' said the agent. 'It is by an American.' He looked at his watch. 'I have to go to the Excelsior,' he said. 'I'll be talking to Rossi again about both of you.'

When he had gone Valentina sighed.

'It will be good if Rossi gets his money soon for this picture from his co-producers,' said the old count. 'In that case he will be able to meet his promissory notes from his last picture.'

'I know about Garibaldi at least,' said Franco.

'Everyone's always going to make a Garibaldi picture,' said the old count. 'Not that they have let this agent of yours read the script, that's obvious. Well, it would have confused him. I have the idea he thinks Garibaldi was an architect who invented Venice.'

Valentina sighed again.

'I wish I was with William Morris,' she said.

'The Morris Agency only want stars,' said Franco. 'Why don't you come swimming with me at the Caesar Augustus? I know an English girl staying there. We can change in her room and go up in the elevator to the pool like guests in the hotel and not pay.'

'No, you go. I'm too cold to swim.'

'If I go by myself, I will have to screw with the English girl,' said Franco. 'I may not get to the pool. I really feel like a swim.'

'Pay, then,' said Valentina. '*Ciao*, Franco.'

When Franco had gone the old count said: 'I am going to my room to read Proust, and then I will have a sleep. Would you like to come and read Proust with me?'

Valentina smiled, leaned back and gazed across at the hotel opposite. Alberto, the doorman, had his summer gloves on. They were a garish optical white, and large. When he gesticulated he looked like Mickey Mouse in them.

'You ought to remember your age sometimes,' said Valentina. 'Really, you can't go on thinking of jumping into bed all the time

like a young man. Maybe I'll come over and read the newspapers
in the lounge, if you want to read your book over there, but anyway, probably Emilio will telephone me.'

In the hotel lounge Valentina said: 'Sometimes I hate acting.
During the entire winter I was in only one commercial. What
sort of a part would I get in this Garibaldi, in any case? A woman
has to do something else. I've asked Emilio more than once: set
me up in a photocopying shop. I'd make it pay in no time at all.
I'm very businesslike. But he won't. He says he'd have to borrow
the money from his wife and she wouldn't lend it to him. But
really it's because he knows I'd make money at it and he'd hate
me to start feeling independent. So here I have this stupid agent
and no work for months.'

'But then Emilio takes you out to dinner in good restaurants,'
said the old count. 'It's very nice if you are a man in the fruit
trade to be able to take an actress about. It's nothing if all he has
to take around is a woman from a photocopy shop. Have you
finished the newspapers, because we could go upstairs?'

'Not really. Anyway, Emilio will probably call. God, I hope I
get this part from Rossi. Did you hear who was to direct?'

'No. Well, I'll see you later. Give my regards to Emilio the
fruit merchant.'

In the evening at the restaurant Franco said: 'I had some
wonderful luck this afternoon.'

'Don't tell me you got a new agent,' said the old count.

'No. You know I wanted to go swimming? Well, it turned out
much better. Naturally, I went and saw the English girl. I had
forgotten how exciting she was, and really she was marvellous for
two whole hours. After that I said I had to go and see my mother,
so I went down in the elevator and bought cigarettes in the lobby
and was just going out when there was this voice: "Franco! How
are you?" and it was this American girl I had seen at Anzio with
some people when we were shooting there, and she'd watched me
acting. A beautiful body. I told her: "Marvellous to see you here,
you look really terrific. Hey, your body really excites me. I just

adore you." And she said: "Why don't you come up to the room
and talk to me?" Another two hours! By then I was starving
hungry.'

'But you didn't take her to dinner.'

'I couldn't afford it. I told her I had to go and see my father in
the hospital. Has Rossi cast the leads in his Garibaldi yet, do you
know? Or did you hear when the shooting is supposed to start?
Someone told me it would be in Spain but someone else said
Israel.'

'Nobody knows who will direct yet for Rossi,' said the old
count. 'The leading actors will never sign until the director is
certain.'

'Maybe by next week,' said Franco hopefully. 'Where's
Valentina this evening?'

'Her friend Emilio came round,' said the old count. 'And this
evening he has taken her out.'

'The boring fruit man!'

'At least he took her out to dinner,' said the old count.

'But fruit! So bourgeois.'

'Naturally, but why not?' said the old count. 'Fruit is very
acceptable to the banks. Old Panone, the distributor, he used to
be in films and fruit, and that was all right with the banks, because
fruit is respectable. Ah, look, there is Aldo, the pimp with the
Mercedes.'

Outside, a large car had arrived and out from it came the young
man Aldo and two girls, pausing to confer a moment before
going up to the apartments next to the restaurant.

'Great looking girls,' said Franco wistfully. 'And he's got a
Mercedes out of it. Maybe I should give up acting and go in for
pimping and get a good car.'

'It is not his Mercedes,' said the old count. 'He is only the
chauffeur. It belongs to an eye surgeon and Aldo drives him about
in the daytime. In the evening the old surgeon and his wife sit at
home out along the Via Flaminia, and they're very kind and let
Aldo take the car home each night so he won't have difficulty

travelling to pick them up in the mornings. They have no idea what he does with it.'

Franco brooded a while and then said: 'Valentina told me she is driving to Marino tomorrow, but not to tell anyone.'

'Ah,' said the old count. 'Then she will be going to see the *mago*. I've told her before not to go, to save her money. So the magician will take her money and do card tricks and pretend to go into a trance. And yet she is a sophisticated woman, she's been in Paris and New York.'

'But she always wants to know her future in films,' said Franco.

'In films or photocopying,' said the old count.

The next evening in the restaurant, Valentina ate her food very briskly, with an air of suppressed exultation. But she didn't say anything till the old count had left the table to go and have a word with Dieter, a blond German actor who had just come back from doing a picture on location. Then she told Franco: 'I had a wonderful day at Marino.'

'With your *mago*?'

'Yes, the *mago*, though he doesn't call himself that. I told him I had a special interest in history at the moment and, do you know, he was able to conjure up the spirit of Mussolini. Why do you smile?'

'You're saying Mussolini talked to you?'

'Through the *mago*, yes. It was absolutely his voice, just like the old newsreels—and the sort of things he used to say, talking to me. *Figlia d'Italia*,' she intoned. '*Ricordi oggi . . .*'

'What's this Daughter of Italy?' asked the old count, suddenly coming back. 'Who called you that?'

'Mussolini,' said Franco. 'At the *mago*'s.'

'That's all I'm telling you,' said Valentina sulkily.

'Your *mago* is obviously a fascist,' said the old count. 'You know, Mussolini once spoke to me. It must have been forty-five years ago. My mother hated him, and he hated her. What a

pompous idiot! I was walking in the Borghese and he came up
riding a horse and asked me: "What are you going to do with
your life, young man?" I said perhaps I might be a writer and he
said very loudly: "I recommend silence." My God, what an
idiot.'

'Anyway, I'm sure it's all a very good omen for the Garibaldi
picture,' said Valentina defiantly.

Dieter came over and joined them and bought them all brandies.
Though German he was unusually popular with everybody,
cheery, generous, and always in work.

'They tell me Piccoli has definitely agreed to direct Rossi's
Garibaldi,' said Dieter. 'Work for everyone, eh?'

'So there you are,' scowled Valentina at the old count.

And indeed it all seemed quite confirmed over the weekend.
On the Monday the Arab agent telephoned both Valentina and
Franco with appointments. Yes, Rossi and Piccoli were definitely
casting now, and would see both of them.

Relaxing after his long location shoot, Dieter had a leisurely
lunch with the old count. 'I used to be frightened what would
happen when it went out of fashion to have the SS as the enemies,'
said Dieter, who had played so many of them that everyone called
him Hitler Youth Dieter. 'But there's always something else they
can think of for me. The Westerns were good while they lasted.
I just used to growl and swear and of course they simply dubbed
everything. It's good being a villain.'

In the evening Valentina was back, radiating confidence.

'Tell me everything,' said the old count. 'You got a part?'

'Yes! A marvellous part, much better than I dreamed. Do they
have roast lamb tonight? I'm having some. My appetite has come
right back. I'm a young bride, just married to a man who joins
Garibaldi's thousand, and I go looking for him. I get four big
scenes. Oh, and one with his corpse—I can make a real meal out
of that.'

'And Franco?'

Valentina made a sad face.

'Poor Franco. Nothing. But he took it well. He's going to Positano. Well, he met a girl at the casting session and she's staying at a villa down there. So I suppose it's not so terrible.'

'So when is the shooting?'

'June, the beginning of June. Six weeks' time. So now that's all settled I can go to my sister and her baby at Subiaco for a few days and relax. Well, the *mago* predicted it, after all.'

'So, full marks to the fascist magician, then,' said the old count.

For the rest of the week the sun shone splendidly, but the rumours came like chill little shadows. Piccoli was not satisfied about the finance. The foreign co-producers had flown in and flown out again, seemingly not satisfied either. There were technical difficulties. By the weekend came firm news. Piccoli had bowed out. Garibaldi was postponed officially for six months.

'With Rossi, postponed is cancelled,' said Franco, back from Positano. 'So, poor Valentina.'

'You look well after Positano,' said the old count. 'Did you swim?'

'A little. Really, it's impossible to be all the time in bed. This girl was Australian, you know. They are always more active than Italian girls.'

And in the evening, the director Piccoli came in to the restaurant with his cameraman Milizia, very late, for a quiet coffee and *sambucca* in a corner. The old count wandered over to them and asked: 'So it's postponed with Rossi, then?'

Piccoli waved a hand wearily. 'Rossi is out,' he announced morosely. 'Well, nobody really needs Garibaldi just now.' He glanced across the room and blinked. '*Ma che bella faccia!* A wonderful face! Is that Dieter?'

'Dieter,' said Milizia. 'He lights very well.'

Piccoli got up and went to sit down with Dieter, all smiles now. '*Caro Dieter!* Listen, are you free? I need you.'

'For Rossi's Garibaldi? What part?'

'No no, Garibaldi's out. A new picture. I'm talking to the French tomorrow. A political picture. Politics and sex—and you are the assassin! The assassin exactly! O.K., tomorrow we fly to Paris. O.K.?'

Valentina next day was plunged into deep gloom. 'I've spots all over my back,' she said. 'And on top of everything else my sister's dog bit me on the ankle.'

'A friend of mine is renting one of the African huts at Tor San Lorenzo,' said the old count. 'There is a kitchen and electricity. It is right on the beach. Here in the city there is too much talk all the time. I am going to the African hut to write some letters. Why don't you come? You can swim all the time in the sea. The water of the sea heals everything.'

'Maybe the spots on my back, but my ruined career? The bite on my ankle?'

'*Everything.*'

PHILIP OAKES

The White Lion

They had seen no-one else all afternoon and at four o'clock the light was going fast. No-one would come now, decided Lomax. It would soon be too dark to shoot and he and his son would go home together. Nothing could be added to the day or taken from it. He would not have to share his pleasure.

The chilly lilac of the autumn sky darkened as they crossed the middle meadow. The boy climbed the fence first and before he followed, Lomax gave him the gun to hold. He swung himself over and smiled at his son.

'Shall we try the spinney?' he said.

'We might see something,' said the boy. He was deliberately casual, showing no excitement and assuming an indifference which he believed to be the correct attitude.

That was the important thing, thought Lomax; to pick a public face and maintain it. What went on behind it was your own affair. You could jump for joy or break your heart, but both were things to do privately. The face you wore outside was chosen for the convenience of others who did not wish to become involved in your affairs and it was also a shell for your own protection. The boy was probably too young to understand that, he thought, but for a child he sized up a situation too well and too fast.

Three pigeons flew into the spinney on their left. They perched low in a tall copper beech and then clumsily hopped to the top of the tree. They were big pale birds that moved with much noise and little grace.

Lomax touched the boy's arm and pointed. 'Try a shot.'

'A sitting target?'

Don't be smug, thought Lomax. 'The light's bad,' he said. 'Bad light and a target at twenty yards makes it fair enough. Take the top one.'

The pigeons had arranged themselves in a triangle and sat separately, nodding like old men in the sun. The boy raised the gun slowly and sighted at the apex. 'Now?'

Lomax nodded. 'Lift it a little. An inch to the right. Squeeze the trigger. Don't pull it.'

The boy corrected himself and fired. There was a puff of feathers as if he had stuck a fork into a bolster, but for a moment the pigeon remained where it was, wedged in the fork of a branch. Then it fell plumply and noisily to the ground. Lomax picked up the bird. Its head fell drunkenly to one side, the eyes were reduced to slits by protective membrane and there was blood on the breast feathers. 'Good shot, Hughie. No worry about that one,' he said.

He put the pigeon in the game bag on top of two rabbits they had shot earlier in the afternoon. 'You can carry the gun,' he said. They climbed the fence and re-crossed the meadow, the bag thumping softly against his thigh at each step. There was a mist softening the tangle of the hawthorn, blue like tobacco smoke, drawing its colour from the last light of the day.

'Byron,' he said aloud. ' "And on the sea a deeper blue and on the leaf a richer hue." Is that how it goes, Hughie?'

'I don't remember,' said the boy.

Lomax felt guilty of an intrusion as if he had tactlessly interrupted a prayer. 'I think that's how it goes,' he said.

He had lost faith in prayer at the age of ten when an hour's supplication beside his bed had failed to produce a desired bicycle. With the other talismans of his youth it had been discarded, no longer potent, and it was not likely to help him now, he thought. He was forty years old, a lean, handsome man with a wife he did not understand and a son he loved dearly. The boy had been conceived on their honeymoon in Spain. Their hotel room had looked out on to a lemon grove. Fruit hung in the trees like wax lanterns and at night they had been kept awake by nightingales and the chorus of frogs which lived in the irrigation ditches. At four in the morning he had gone out on to the balcony, his bare flesh crinkling in the chill and shouted at the frogs to be quiet.

'For God's sake,' said Kate. 'Come back to bed.'

'I can't stand their bloody noise.'

She stretched luxuriously. 'I don't mind it.'

'I can't sleep. I'll be useless tomorrow.'

'It's tomorrow already,' she said. 'Don't worry about it. Come and make love to me.'

'That's your answer to everything.'

'There are worse answers.'

'I'm sure there are,' he said bitterly. 'Not that they'd interest you.'

'Was it that bad?' she asked. 'It wasn't for me.'

He did not answer immediately, then shook his head. 'I was never much good at that sort of thing. I'm sorry.'

'Sorry?' she said. 'Stop being so bloody British. I've told you. It was all right.' She got out of bed and stood behind him. He felt her warmth against his back, but before she could embrace him he stepped away.

'I think I'll take a pill,' he said.

'Please yourself.'

Her flat voice angered him. 'I may as well. I obviously can't please you.'

'Of course you please me.'

He shook his head as though he was flicking off beads of sweat. It was useless, he thought. He could not begin to explain his pain or his exasperation. His performance had been absurd, the fumbling of a clumsy amateur. He was humiliated and indirectly he blamed her for excusing him, as if experience gave her the right to patronise. When she put her hands on his shoulders and tried to turn him to face her, he jabbed backwards with his elbow and felt it collide with her breast. 'I didn't mean to do that,' he said.

'I think you did.' She leaned against the door, both hands covering the bruise.

'If I hurt you, I'm sorry.'

'Don't apologise. Just take your pill.'

He had, in fact, taken two and when he awoke it was mid-morning and the frogs and the nightingales were silent. For the rest of the honeymoon they had been careful with each other, nurturing every courtesy, taking care not to disagree until their anxiety not to offend became more worrying than the offence itself. And so it had continued and Lomax had learned to look for small returns, arming himself against disappointment, remaining on guard, charily accepting a state of siege.

He stumbled over a molehill as they crossed the meadow and deliberately slackened pace. He did not want to lose any of the day by hurrying its end. All stages had to be passed and experienced and there was always richness in the last minute. The boy walked beside him, the rifle in the crook of his arm and Lomax glanced at him secretly, delighting in their physical resemblance. He had no look of Kate about him, not that such a likeness would be a disadvantage, Lomax admitted. Kate was an attractive woman, small but strong, with a fine silky skin that felt too smooth, too delicate to protect her flesh. She was not fat, but her body was sturdy like that of a small child, oddly tender but knowing. She had glossy brown hair, a wide mouth and short-sighted grey eyes. Lomax had not been the first of her lovers and he wondered occasionally whether he would be the last or if indeed there was already someone else.

He and Kate quarrelled often, or rather he quarrelled and she allowed the quarrel to proceed, remaining in the room until he had exhausted his sarcasm and then quietly leaving. She would have been entitled to find someone else, thought Lomax. They had not ceased to love each other, but an accumulation of resentment and old hurts burdened them like underwater insects and made their progress towards each other awkward and impractical.

The game bag thudded softly against his leg. 'Think you can skin a rabbit?' he asked the boy.

'I can try,' said Hughie without turning his head. He had tried before, willing to learn but stiff-fingered under his father's surveillance. The flesh and fur had refused to part and he had panicked when blood made his hands greasy. His father had said nothing but had taken the rabbit from him and completed the skinning, stripping back the pelt from the pearly ligament, demonstrating the speed and ease with which it could be done.

'There's more to shooting than firing a rifle,' he told the boy. 'It's no use knowing only half a job.'

There was a correct way to carry the gun, a procedure to follow in cleaning it, a method of oiling to be learned; in fact, a gap to be bridged between the lax amateur world and the cool proficiency of the professional. Lomax was a professional and amateurs bored him. As an account executive with an advertising agency he knew that a campaign, however inspired, was valueless without the muscle of an organisation behind it, checking and implementing detail, spelling out the message again and again until the connection had been made. Unconsciously he thought in slogans. 'Do it well if you do it at all.' 'Always make your effort the maximum.' And because he believed the precepts to be true he obeyed them implicitly. He was not ingenuous, however, and he was not insensitive. Kate had accused him of coldness but Lomax knew that he was capable of loving with a concentration that was beyond her. She was demonstrative and untidy in her affections. He could not bear to see her fondling the boy, afraid that she would soften him and infect him with her own emotional disarray. He wanted only the best for his son and his contribution to the boy's welfare was to equip him for the world in which he would live. The professional fared better than the amateur and Hughie had to learn how to survive.

Lomax had schooled himself not to look for affection, but

sometimes he was saddened by the distance between himself and his son. He longed for companionship, an alliance. He educated himself in subjects which he thought would interest a boy. He bought record albums which he detested. He put up with cricket which he had always regarded as a waste of time. He tried to teach Hughie how to swim but the boy was afraid of the water and would not trust his father to support him. It was obvious that of his parents he preferred Kate and regarded Lomax with some-thing that was close to fear. His demands made the boy nervous and unsure of himself. The pace he set was too fast.

They reached the road and walked down the long avenue of trees to where he had left the car. The sky was a deep, clear purple and the air was frosty. Lomax drove home fast and expertly, swinging the car round the narrow lanes and passing through the white gateposts of his own garden without slowing down. Hughie jumped out of the car and opened the garage doors, then without waiting for his father ran into the house. Lomax locked the garage and followed him stiffly.

He took off his boots in the kitchen and sat wearily for several minutes, staring at the mud on his fingers. He washed his hands and went into the living-room. There was a bright fire burning and Kate sat on the floor surrounded by a litter of magazines. She had her arm round the boy's shoulders and he was talking to her excitedly.

'Did he tell you he made a good shot?' asked Lomax.

Kate nodded. 'He'll be shooting lions next.'

'A white lion,' said Hughie.

'To make a bedside rug for me,' said Kate, stroking his hair.

Lomax felt like a visitor to the house, not conversant with the family jokes. 'Why a white lion?' he asked foolishly.

Kate laughed and put her arm around Hughie's shoulders. 'It's just a story,' she said. 'One that we made up.'

Lomax knew about the omnibus stories invented by Kate and Hughie, a new chapter being added each night before Hughie went to sleep. One concerned a small boy, Hughie himself, who could see through walls with one magic eye. Another was about a far country ruled by scarlet birds where the rocks spouted lemonade and the palaces were lit by glow-worms. Another introduced a prospector who found buried treasure and re-interred it because he thought gold a wholly impractical metal.

Lomax felt ill at ease in their fantasies. 'Make the stories more like life,' he suggested.

'But that would bore me,' said Kate. 'I see quite enough of life as it is and there's time enough for Hughie to come to grips with it.'

She was quite calm but Lomax felt that she was erecting barricades and drawing a line in the dust which he was forbidden to cross. He could not guess what would happen if he crossed the line but he knew that he was being warned away.

Kate smoothed the boy's hair and Lomax was suddenly jealous. 'Tell me about the lion,' he commanded.

'It's just a white lion,' said Hughie reluctantly, looking to Kate for confirmation.

Lomax attempted a smile. 'Where does it live?'

'No special place,' said Hughie, tracing a pattern in the carpet with his finger. 'In the garden sometimes.'

'Our garden?'

Hughie nodded. 'In the garden and in the meadow but not everyone can see it. It's invisible to most people.' He gave the facts grudgingly, as if defending his private world.

'Is it big?' Lomax asked.

'Big and strong,' said Hughie. 'No one can catch it.'

'But you were going to shoot it.'

Hughie looked at him pityingly. 'That was a joke,' he said. 'I wouldn't shoot it.'

'Not even for a bedside rug?'

The boy shook his head and smiled down at the carpet.

'I wouldn't want him to,' said Kate.

'I would,' said Lomax. 'I'd like to see it stretched out, here and now, as flat as a pancake.' He gripped Hughie's chin. 'Show it to me,' he said. 'I'll shoot it.'

'You wouldn't see it,' said Hughie. 'It would stay invisible.'
He spoke serenely, certain that the lion was safe.

Lomax gripped the boy's arm. 'Listen to me. I wouldn't see it
because it doesn't exist. There is no lion. You must know the
difference between what's real and make-believe. The lion's just
part of a story.'

'I've seen it,' said Hughie.

Kate pushed him towards the door. 'Go and wash your hands,'
she said. 'Let's forget about lions.' She looked warningly at
Lomax.

'I've seen it,' said Hughie. 'It has white fur and yellow eyes. I
saw it in the garden.'

'You're telling deliberate lies now,' said Lomax sharply. 'You
can't tell the difference between truth and fiction.' He stood up,
determined to settle the issue between them finally and at once.
'Make up your mind now. You imagined the lion.'

'It was in the garden last night,' said Hughie. 'I saw it by the
fish-pond.'

Deliberately Lomax slapped his face on either side, rocking the
boy with the force of the blows. 'You imagined it,' he said.

Kate caught his arm and stepped in front of Hughie. 'Go on,'
she said, 'he won't do that again.'

'I will if I think it necessary,' said Lomax.

'No,' said Kate. 'No you won't.' She put her arm round her
son and guided him upstairs.

Lomax walked slowly into the kitchen where the rifle stood in
a corner. The windows showed him his own reflection, the white
tiled walls, the stripped pine dresser, the Aga and the electric
clock. There was no-one else in the room and no sound except
the dripping of the cold water tap, but for a long time he
stood listening for the tick of claws on the cork floor and the
immortal breath of the creature that possessed his house.

PAUL THEROUX

The Scrimshaw Oracle

Afterwards, Bishop Brain could not contemplate his napkin ring without repressing a feeling of disgust and horror. The origin of this singular revulsion was in consequence of a period of bone idleness during which he agreed to search for a parishioner, one Joe Yurkus, who had vanished in California. In pursuit of Yurkus, the kindly bishop found himself travelling incognito on what he quickly gathered was a beat-the-clock plane flight from Boston to San Francisco. His seatmate, whose hindparts he noted with disquiet were sausaged into a pair of jeans superscribed with the name of a millionairess, promptly announced herself as an actress. Her eyes displayed the electric glare of lunacy, and her luggage-tag the words, *Constance Reader*.

Constance Reader, in cruel defiance of her name, was dyslexic. It seemed an unfortunate handicap in an actress, but she was swift in pointing out that she was a member of a mime troupe and, such were the exigencies of her profession, had 'occasionally moonlighted in corsets', by which she meant wholesaled surgical goods. This brought forth from the bishop the story of Joe Yurkus, for Yurkus too had been travelling in surgical goods and had been last sighted in the Carmel area, where Miss Reader herself lived. The bishop realized that he must have sounded pretty passionate on the subject of Yurkus's disappearance because, after he explained the nature of his quest, his seatmate shot forth, 'Golly, you must really care about him!'

'Reader, I married him,' the bishop said gravely.

The actress's jaw dropped mimetically and it was left to the prelate to make the elaborate explanation: the source of the quotation (he had recklessly forgotten her dyslexia), the ceremony he had performed as a curate at St Stephen's, and the unhappy end of Yurkus's marriage when Mrs Y. urgently became possessed of a desire to 'get in touch with her feelings'. The bishop had fully intended to introduce himself as a salesman of slogans for bumper stickers—not the usual ones, of which *I'd Rather Be Sailing* was lamentably typical, but mottoes from Thomas Hardy, Mark Twain, Olive Schreiner and Thomas Babington Macaulay. But now Constance Reader, who had proved to be wilfully illiterate, knew the truth about him. For his part, he conceded that her ignorance had proved a greater stratagem than his ill-timed knowingness, and he reminded himself that you could not be too careful.

'Where is your facility located?' the actress inquired in hearty tones.

'You mean, my church?' the bishop guessed drily.

'Not only church, but church-type resources and related stuff.'

'The Boston archdiocese,' the bishop said softly. 'I'm afraid St Stephen's is not what it was. I can remember—oh, years ago— when we'd have a full house, all praying for the conversion of Russia. Maybe it's me,' he continued, 'but it seems vouchsafing has fallen off considerably.'

'People aren't interested in spiritual inputs,' observed the actress.

It forcefully struck the bishop that statements of this kind had allowed the rejoinder, 'You can say that again' to pass quietly into obsolescence.

'This Yurkus,' she went on hastily, 'he's probably set himself up in business in the Carmel area. He could have impacted there, making yogurt or sandals.'

The bishop, wildly anxious lest she see his smirk, turned away and addressed the troposphere through the plane window. 'He

wasn't the yogurt or sandals type,' he said of his enterprising
parishioner. 'No, surgical goods seem to have been more his line,
though I admit there's a little confusion on this point. His sister
was firmly of the belief that he intended to retail bakery goods
and some kind of confectionery.'

'Industrial software's a no-no in Carmel,' was the actress's
reply, 'but you could do a dynamite business in bakery goods and
confectionery. Was he laid back?'

The bishop was prepared for this interjection. Californians, he
knew, said 'laid back' because they were unacquainted with its
much bubblier synonym 'imperturbable'.

'Yes,' assented Bishop Brain. 'Which makes it all the more
mysterious that his sister is unshakably certain that he—that he—
I don't,' confessed the bishop, 'know quite how to put this—'

But Constance Reader was quickly to discern the solemnity on
his face and said unsmilingly, 'You mean, you think he's in an
in-ground situation?'

'Exactly,' sighed the bishop.

Some hours later it was the actress's turn to address the plane
window. 'There's a whole bunch of water down there!' she
exclaimed, her blue eyes a binocular echo of the Pacific Ocean.

The bishop's offer of a ride accepted by the actress with keenness
and a flicker of awe, they betook themselves to a car rental agency
and were soon, knees against the subcompact's dashboard, head-
ing south for Carmel. To while away the time, the bishop regaled
her with samples of his apron slogans (*Heaven for the Weather, Hell
for the Company*, was one that particularly amused her) and she
rewarded him with her gauche sophistication. She spoke of
buying 'grosheries' and being 'matoor' and she mentioned New
York crudity with a palm on her pained 'four-head'. Yet, in spite
of high spirits, she could not dispel the suggestion of mounting
menace in the bishop's mind about the fate of Joe Yurkus. As
they motored on, he felt increasingly uneasy. He did not like these

bosomy hills, and every Hispanically-named town seemed an occasion of sin. The pair stopped in Castroville to lunch on artichokes, the principal crop in the area which proclaimed itself 'The Artichoke Capital of the World'—it seemed an irredeemable solecism not to say 'Heart'. His were marinated, hers deep-fried. The actress was greatly taken by their size, and this put the bishop in mind of one of his apron mottoes.

'So big,' he remarked gravely, 'that it only takes eleven of them to make a dozen.'

It had only been a chance remark, but for the next hour or two the actress seemed to labour under a burden of frowning perplexity.

By that time they had sped through Monterrey and, chiefly to avoid the freeway, driven through the Pebble Beach promontory, noting signs. One sign had not failed to catch Bishop Brain's eye: *No Fishing, No Camping, No Abaloning.* It was not an East Coast verb—he was not sure it was a verb at all—but it gave him another motto to augment his case of samples: *I'd Rather Be Abaloning.*

Carmel was blossoms and then, in just the same fashion that one's eyes grow accustomed to the dark, he could see that beneath the blossoms and behind them were hundreds of tiny houses, calculated to look tumbledown and scarcely visible, yet in a kind of pristine state of dilapidation which had its eastern counterpart in 'weathered' siding. That is to say, there was not a wormhole out of place, and every swaybacked roof looked as premeditated and explicit as if decreed by an architect. This cosy decrepitude and toy-town hauteur was not new to the bishop—after all, he had blessed the fleet in Provincetown—but the pompous miniaturization spoke volumes, and he quickly grasped that, yes, they bought 'grosheries' here, too.

He became creepily conscious that unobscured by the Munchkin nature of the houses was a kind of hoggish wealth. It took all his ecclesiastical forbearance to refrain from thinking of it as loot, dividends and widows' booty. The street-signs, variously Spanish and British, seemed alarmingly incongruous, Las Tiendas Court hard by Tuck Box Court, like a Zapata mustache on a stiff upper-lip. Like many another easterner, he was impressed by a California style which seemed arbitrary without being authoritative and by municipal design that seemed less city-planning than self-satire.

Constance Reader took this all in her stride and, enjoined by the bishop to assist him in his quest for his missing parishioner, she at once agreed, suggesting by the way that they base themselves at a hotel called Pancho Villa, her own condominium being too far from town to make sleuthing convenient.

'I have a queen-sized bed with water-views,' the hotel manager offered, and with exasperated archness added, 'I take it the lady is sharing.'

'Separate rooms,' was the bishop's chaste response.

Routinely rummaging in his bathroom, Bishop Brain came across a lozenge of fenestrated plastic and, discovering it to be air-freshener, turned it over and saw a message which seemed to him on reflection to be worthy of a minor metaphysical poet. 'Please replace,' it urged, 'when contents have shrunk to a small dark mass.'

And this roused him to action, for it overwhelmingly put him in mind of poor Yurkus.

'Telling his sister that he's going to sell surgical goods,' the bishop quietly elaborated to Constance Reader at the secluded hearth of the Pancho Villa, while a Duraflame log purred tamely in chemical crepitation on the grate, 'he comes to Carmel and changes his story. Now it's confectionery and bakery goods. He apparently sets up some sort of business in a local arcade—The Shambles, I've just found it on the Chamber of Commerce map— and begins to send his sister what she calls "California-type letters". That is, desperate messages on Peanuts notepaper. At first she thinks he's describing the weather. "It's getting hot here," and so forth. But soon they appear to be descriptions of harassment. I quote: "They're making it hot for me here." I don't intend to shock you, Miss Reader, with his graphic stories

of persecution, but let me say that soon the letters stopped
entirely and it is assumed that he has either taken a header into the
Pacific or been done-in in what his sister believes is a "California-
type way".'

'Stiffed,' the actress whispered, while at the same time admiring
the mutters of combustion in the hearth. 'And maybe by someone
in the same racket.'

'Precisely,' was the bishop's opinion. But the actress's dark
suggestion of a rival implicated very nearly everyone in the
flower bedecked town, for investigation confirmed that a perambulation of just one street brought them within view of twenty
shops retailing home-made varieties of gingersnaps and fudge.
Apart from wickerwork handbags and hideous gouaches—and of
course aprons and T-shirts printed with unimaginative mottoes—
the town sold nothing else. For simplicity's sake, the bishop
eliminated all those shopkeepers as suspects, but he retained a
general impression of the Carmel populace. They were of a certain
age, but they had a snap in them, the shine of health that told you
that they had, in the course of their lives, taken their toe off the
bottom and done marvellously. It seemed an even greater mystery
that Joe Yurkus had believed he could succeed there, for he had
been a strapping, raw-boned fellow, six feet from the hole in his
sock to the visor of his (*Yankee Surgicals*) baseball cap, and the
shabby shapelessness of his habitual working clothes was thoroughly at odds with the golfer's garb (red trousers, white shoes,
monogrammed blazer) of these twinkling mountebanks.

He had been saving The Shambles for last, but on the morning
he was to make his visit, Constance Reader was edgy at breakfast.
She said she did not think she would accompany him today. The
inconclusiveness of the search had given her intimations ('flashes'
was her word) of the frustrations of her own assorted careers, as a
failed medical student, an unsuccessful surgical-goods salesperson
and dyslexic actress. The bishop said he was deeply sorry, and he
went on to explain that he held the view that word-blindness
sharpened the other senses.

The actress was momentarily emboldened, then in apologetic tones reiterated her reluctance. 'Know what I need?' she said, raising her elbows and flapping them slightly, duck-like, and yet in perfect mimicry of a painting Bishop Brain had once seen in the Louvre, *The Threatened Swan*, 'That.'

'I understand,' was the bishop's reply. 'Elbow room.'

'Personal space,' corrected the actress.

So he went alone, to Joe Yurkus's last known address, where the missing Bostonian had reportedly sold confectionery and bakery goods. This was The Shambles, just off Fox and Grapes Court. As a precaution, the bishop had brought his case of samples: the apron and T-shirt mottoes.

'Help you?' An apple-cheeked dowager in a pinafore hurried forward. *Scrimshaw* said the sign above her head, and in the windows of her shop the handicrafts she proudly displayed, fine-worked designs of ships and chipmunks and Carmel's own cypresses on napkin rings and paperweights. Yurkus's shop, under new management.

Bishop Brain introduced himself as a salesman of new-fangled apron mottoes and delivered what he like to think of as his spiel, with an apt and very selling quotation from *Jude the Obscure*. The woman divulged that her name was Mrs Musprat and that she was thrilled to bits.

'You've got to meet Dora,' she said, applying her knuckles to the shop-window next door.

The bishop was encouraged to see the woman in question, Dora Haddy by name, emerge from a shop selling the very aprons he himself was attempting to boost, the great difference being that her wares were the old familiar, *Who Invited All These Tacky People?* and *My Mom and Dad Went To Carmel and All They Bought Me Was This Dumb T-Shirt*.

Mrs Musprat said, 'Dora, you're going to like this guy.'

He explained his approach to apron and T-shirt mottoes, all the while taking the measure of the two shop-keepers, and after he had finished, the women chorused, employing a locution characteristic of California, 'You're neat!'

This was, Bishop Brain knew well, the highest accolade. The question in his mind was so thoroughly rehearsed that out it came without a cautionary prologue.

'Does the name Joe Yurkus mean anything to you?' was the bishop's swift inquiry.

Mrs Musprat blanched, Mrs Haddy blinked, but before he could, as it were, wrong-foot them with another question, they protested that neither of them had ever heard the name. Their protestation was suggestive of a secret bitterness.

The bishop went on to describe the missing Yurkus, and this brought forth a distinct shudder of revulsion in Mrs Musprat and a stammer in Mrs Haddy's eyelids.

'We don't,' advanced Mrs Musprat suddenly, 'have that sort of person around here.'

'He was apparently selling confectionery and bakery goods,' the bishop put in.

Why are they laughing at this? the bishop reflected, and why is their laughter just the teeniest bit hysterical? He was going to continue his impromptu cross-examination, but he was thwarted by a crowd of browsers, some admiring Mrs Musprat's scrimshaw and others, in stage whispers, reading the ludicrous slogans on Mrs Haddy's aprons and T-shirts. In despair at this turn of events, Bishop Brain purchased a napkin ring which, though hardly a snip at twenty-five dollars, allowed him to engage the woman in further conversation about the acorn motif scrimshawed upon it.

And yet, before he had time to utter Yurkus's name once more, Mrs Musprat expostulated, 'I've got to mulch my rhodies!' and sprinted on sneakered feet to her car where Bishop Brain's breathless urgencies were terminated by the slam of her car door. His instinct, so quickly does disguise insinuate itself upon reality, was to look at her bumper-sticker. *Save The Whales* it implored.

'A hunch, nothing more,' the bishop explained without gesticu-

lation back at Pancho Villa's Sticky Wicket Tea Shoppe over a
plate of iced fancies. Constance Reader listened politely, and yet
her glazed stare betrayed nothing but muddle and inattention.
Distractingly, she had pushed her sunglasses back, so they rested
on her hair. They wear them on their heads here, was the bishop's
grave reflection, as he continued to relate the details of his
encounter with the two odd women at The Shambles.

'They sound neat,' was the actress's rejoinder, and the bishop
concluded that she had missed his point entirely—missed it
perhaps because she was so determinedly punishing a tea-cake.

'I think I've got a suspect,' the prelate said meditatively, 'but
in the meantime,' he went on, lowering his eyes, 'I've also got a
pair of sore feet. They used to refer to policemen as flatfoots,' he
recalled. 'Now I know why!'

'You ought to get some cookies,' the actress said between bites.
'They're neat for propping you up.'

The bishop had to smile at this, and with exquisite condes-
cension he stated, 'I have passed the stage where—do they still
call them Oreos?—are capable of improving my morale.'

'Not that kind,' the actress said. 'The kind you put in your
shoes for support—those lumpy things. "Cookies" is what
they're called in the trade. You forgot,' she elaborated, 'that I
was into surgical goods! Hey,' she remembered, 'wasn't this guy
Yurkus—?'

The actress had, all this time, been removing one of the items
in question, a 'cookie', from one of her own pumps, and she held
the malodorous object for the bishop to verify as she persisted in
her interrogation.

His features pinched, the bishop cut her short with, 'If that's
what cookies are, what is candy?'

'There's all sorts of candy,' the actress said lightly, but with
decided ambiguity.

'I mean,' the bishop persevered, 'the candy that isn't confectionery. What sort of candy would you buy at a surgical goods
shop, the sort of surgical goods shop that sells foot-cookies?'

'I've known facilities,' the actress explained, 'that sold sink candy, cistern candy and,' tracing the products with finger movements that suggested shapes, using all her abilities as a mimic to elucidate the knowledge she had gained as a surgical salesperson, 'urinal candy.'

The bishop just managed to repeat the horribly bewitching name. 'Urinal candy?' he gasped.

'Those little deodorizing discs that you see in the trough of the facility that men—what's wrong?'

'It all adds up,' the bishop said, squinting. 'Confectionery and bakery goods—that's what Yurkus's sister said. Simple misapprehension. He had said cookies and candy, but of course in Carmel, such unthinkable—' A note of resolution entered the bishop's voice. 'We've got a motive,' he calculated. 'We've got a suspect. Why, we even have a victim!' Glumness overtook him. 'What is lacking in this case,' he concluded, 'is a corpse. Yurkus disappeared into thin air!'

It was at that moment, nervously fingering the napkin ring he had bought from Mrs Musprat's, that the bishop withdrew it from his pocket where he had been toying with it, and offered it to the gaze of the actress.

'Neat,' was her judgement.

'Scrimshaw,' the bishop said carelessly. 'They make them from whales' teeth, that kind of thing. Quite an art, all that scratching. And that's the funny thing. Mrs Musprat, the lady who's responsible for this, has a *Save The Whales* bumper sticker on her car. Rather bad taste, I should say. And the contradiction can't help but make you suspicious. *She's* not saving any whales!'

'Yes, she is,' the actress said, and expertly examined the napkin ring with a heartless calm that reminded the bishop of her disclosure that she had dropped out of medical school. She returned the napkin ring to its owner and pronounced, 'This piece of scrimshaw, as you call it, is a human bone.'

'I wish,' the bishop said, avoiding contact with the thing that lay before him, 'I really wish I could go back to The Shambles and confront those two sweet old ladies. But I don't have the backbone.'

'Well, this is a start,' the actress said, snatching up the napkin ring once more. And with a certainty in her voice that seemed to the bishop to come straight from the dissection room she said, 'It happens to be a thoracic vertebra.'

Neither Mrs Musprat nor Mrs Haddy was contrite about the murder they had carried out. They did not gloat, but they did maintain that they had rid the lovely town of a dangerous person. And they confirmed that once he had begun selling 'cookies' and 'candy' they had decided to do him in. It was some time after this that Mrs Musprat had taken up scrimshaw. Now she was very good at it, she said, but she confessed to the bishop that the basic material was in short supply. It seemed to the bishop a wholly unlikely setting for a rehearsal of Burke and Hare, but the widows looked at him and his companion with such enterprising eyes that he prudently withdrew. Shortly afterwards, Constance Reader, now thoroughly chastened, comprised all that there was of a congregation as, interceding on behalf of the murderesses, Bishop Brain used the Carmel Mission to say a small dark Mass.

DAVID GALEF

Robertson

Robertson was released from the ward the week after Thanks-giving. Walking down the block with his bundle of personal belongings under his arm, he saw a shop window display of a larger-than-life turkey that remained from the holiday. Seeing the plastic feast behind the glass made him recall the sudsy taste of the mashed potatoes at the institutional Thanksgiving meal. It also made him think about how hungry he was. Institution meals had always been provided three times a day, at specified hours. Here it was five o'clock in the afternoon with no one to bring a tray around; there was none of the carefully worked-out routine that marked the time. Dr Renshaw had mentioned a period of readjustment.

Naturally, as part of the out-patient procedure, Robertson would be checked on from time to time, but assistance was supposed to be minimal, to see if he could stand on his own two feet. He looked at his feet as they walked down the sidewalk for him. Each step was slightly tentative, and he felt uneasy every time he avoided stepping on a crack in the sidewalk. He was supposed to be over all that by now, though bits of old behaviour patterns would always remain. To compromise, he deliberately stepped on a crack every fourth or fifth step, but that gave him the same nervous feeling after a while.

He walked uptown until he got to a residential apartment district not too far from a lot of cheap-looking stores. He had

written down a list of things to do right away, and the item that
headed the list, in painfully neat block capitals, was to find himself
a room. Then, get something to eat, get a job. Before his illness,
he had been a proof reader for a small publishing firm that put
out expensively bound reprints. He wondered idly whether he
would get back his old job, even though he had given no notice
of his quitting when he had left the time before.

Three hours later, he was inelegantly twirling spaghetti in a place
called Pastaria four blocks from his new home. The apartment he
had rented was on the third floor: two small rooms, with a
kitchenette and a tiny bathroom. It wasn't furnished very well,
and there was only a drab view of the street, but it was in a
comparatively quiet section of the city. Peculiarly, after all the
enforced quiet in the hospital, what he wanted was still more
quiet, but at his own choice, rather than at the request of some
nurse. Dawdling over a small cup of spumoni, he reviewed his
situation once more: he was out of a job for the moment, but
would probably soon be employed. He had about seven hundred
dollars' time in which to do it; if he was lucky, he might even be
able to regain his old job at the publishing company. It was quite
important that he get his former job, live in the same type of
neighbourhood in which he had lived before, and cultivate the
same habits. It was his way of re-establishing security. On his
way back to the apartment, he walked into an all-night drug store
and bought a book of crossword puzzles. Just as he was leaving
the store, he remembered he had nothing to write with, so he
went back in to buy a cheap ball-point pen, which he made the
clerk try out before it was acceptable.

He spent the rest of the evening checking out the apartment,
looking into corners, testing the mattress, and setting up his few
personal belongings. If he hadn't been in such a hurry to find a
place for the night, he would have looked around longer: the
rooms were dirty and the heat was bad. He needed a broom and

some towels, and dozens of other articles to put in the bathroom, the kitchen, and the bedroom. He had a definite conception of how he wanted things arranged in the apartment, and he planned a few specific chores to do the next day—after he got a job; the job was the main thing. Lying on the bed, with the sheets that smelled indefinably of previous tenancy, he filled in a crossword puzzle, leaving one square blank because he had forgotten one of the standard clues. He went to sleep anyway, but at two o'clock in the morning he got out of bed, filled in the last square, and went back to sleep. Four-letter word for an Anglo-Saxon serf, *esne*.

He woke later than he had intended, so the first item he bought on his shopping rounds was an alarm clock. Unable to present himself at the door of his old employer smartly and sharply at nine o'clock, he slouched in at eleven-thirty, only to find that the firm had moved to another part of the city. Oddly enough, another publishing firm had taken over the occupancy, and Robertson decided to ask for a job. He gave them a quick story about his being new in the city, which they may or may not have believed, but he proofed a galley to their satisfaction, and they engaged him in place of the temporary help they had been using. The pay was low, but the work was what Robertson knew, and he was happy to get a position so similar to his old one that fast. Briefly elated, he went shopping for a mountain of items for use in the apartment. During the afternoon, he located a better restaurant than Pastaria in the neighbourhood. Then he spent some time arranging and subtly rearranging the items in the rooms to fit his picture of his old apartment. Before going to sleep, he filled in another crossword puzzle.

A few weeks passed, and he began to get settled in his situation. The apartment became hospitable to him, even though the landlord had agreed to have the walls redone in what turned out to be an unattractive dead white. He spent much of his time reading mediocre paperbacks anyway, and didn't pay much attention to

his surroundings or any of the neighbouring tenants. It was as
though, once he had made sure he was comfortable, the question
was settled for good. He often cooked for himself in the cramped
kitchenette, but only simple dishes, and he always cleaned up
promptly afterwards, so that the apartment, in general, always
looked as if the last tenant had suddenly died, and nothing had
been moved yet.

His job at the publishing firm continued as it had in his previous
employment: as he demonstrated his competence at ferreting out
errors, he was allowed to do minor editing, the usual stock-in-
trade of the minor employee. He had never bothered to look up
the old publishing firm; now that he had another job, it wasn't
worth the embarrassment of returning, hat in hand—he didn't
even own a hat. He made enough money to pay the monthly rent
punctually, live fairly cheaply, and have a bit left over for savings.

In late December, he received a notice from the clinic asking that
he make an appointment at the earliest convenience. The only
contact he had made with the people at the clinic was a brief note
advising them of his new address and job; the requested recall
irked him peculiarly. Of course, he had been aware that they
would be checking up on him. He knew it was just a formality,
but it was a suggestion, just a hint, that he wasn't quite well yet.
With five more days to Christmas, among green and red electric
signs in the shop windows, he walked forty blocks to the hospital,
where he waited half an hour in a secretary's office before going in
to see Dr Renshaw.

Seated behind a desk which showed a broad expanse of polished
wood, Dr Renshaw rose to shake Robertson's hand. Renshaw
was a short, silvery man in his fifties who dressed conservatively.
He habitually shook hands with his patients, Robertson remembered, though he used to wonder whether Renshaw did this by
habit or whether it was some form of therapy. In any case, he
pretended that he didn't notice the proffered hand and sat down

in the chair by the side of the desk. Dr Renshaw grinned weakly
and asked him how he was, how his job was working out, how
he liked his apartment, and so on. Robertson answered briefly
and without interest. His chief concern was to get the interview
over with and get the hell out: being back in the hospital stirred
up unpleasant memories. Dr Renshaw, underneath his mild
questioning, might have been trying to bring them back.

Renshaw asked him what he was doing these days, what kept
him interested. 'I see you're still carrying around your crossword
puzzle book—still hooked, eh?'

'I do one a day.'

Renshaw gestured at the *Penny Crosswords No. 12* Robertson
had jammed in his coat pocket. 'Nothing wrong with a hobby or
two, keeps the boredom away—how are your other habits?' The
tone of voice was still easy; Renshaw leaned forward as if he
hadn't discomfited Robertson enough already—and looked a
little startled. Chiefly, he was staring at the revealed upper half of
the book in Robertson's pocket.

'Would—would you mind . . . um, could I see your book for a
second?'

He didn't give a reason, and Robertson passed it over in
silence. Renshaw flipped through the book as if fascinated,
though he glanced back from time to time at Robertson.

'Well, ah, keep at it,' he said finally, though the smile was
forced. 'How about not stepping on cracks, or keeping your
hands clean—that still bother you at all?'

To his surprise, Robertson found himself raising his voice
quite high: 'Look, can we just get this questioning over with? I
didn't want to come here in the first place.'

Renshaw bit his lip; Robertson sensed the doctor was uneasily
remaining quiet about something, which was fine with him. Anything to finish the questioning sooner. If he had known it was
going to be like this, he wouldn't have come. He thought he knew
exactly what Renshaw was referring to: little behaviour quirks,
like not walking on sidewalk cracks or filling in crosswords

perfectly in pen had obsessed him long before his collapse, though Renshaw insisted on referring to it as an 'episode'.

Renshaw probed a bit more, and Robertson made a few vague replies, mostly repetitions of his earlier statements about how he felt he was adjusting well and was getting used to his job again. Suggesting, but not violently insisting, that you were happy was a good way to stop the questions, he knew. Renshaw probably saw through the blind, but listened calmly to it all. At times, he seemed awfully curious about Robertson's day-to-day routine. The rest of the interview was brief. Renshaw jotted down a few particulars in his notebook and got up to see him out. At the door, Renshaw suddenly became quite frank: he laid a hand on Robertson's shoulder and told him that he still exhibited signs of stress; he mentioned something about restful routine.

Robertson kept the understanding smile on his face through the hospital corridors and for two blocks afterward, just for practice, thinking all the while how much he disliked Dr Renshaw. Renshaw, he decided, must have a particularly diseased and paranoid mind to see symptoms in so many people. The thought made him feel a little better, and by the time he reached his apartment, he felt superior.

He walked up the stairs to his apartment: three flights, the same level his old apartment had been on. Once inside, he flopped down on the bed and read for a while. In a few hours, it would be time for dinner, and he would get out the chopped meat from the refrigerator. He had always liked hamburgers, and he had them on Tuesdays and Thursdays. The routine was deeply imbedded enough so that it wasn't quite clear whether he knew it was Tuesday or Thursday, and so bought chopped meat—or whether the presence of the chopped meat in the refrigerator reminded him what day it was. He was as reasonably happy with his existence as he suspected he ever would be.

Walking home from the clinic that night, Dr Renshaw turned over the facts in the Robertson case and came up with the same opinion each time. Granted, the interview had shown the man to be still nervous and somewhat sullen, but he had adjusted, and eventually even the nervous traces after the breakdown would disappear. Robertson would become again one of thousands of entirely forgettable men working at obscure jobs in the city. His need to return to his old life wasn't all that unusual; few people ever made 'new beginnings'. Still, Robertson's case struck Renshaw as unique and slightly eerie. He paused at the curbside, thinking of the one clue which showed what Robertson had done: the crossword puzzle book he had brought with him to the interview had been the same one he had brought with him just after the collapse—*all filled in*, and then gone over in another pen. All Robertson had told him about the new routine made it abundantly clear that what he had done was to make sure that everything—exactly everything—was the way it had been before. Filling in the little secure squares of life.

The significance of such a choice at the same time appalled and relieved Renshaw. It was bizarre; there was something surreal to living out your life in a circle, to the minutest details. Robertson had even managed to buy the same grey jacket he wore a year before. No doubt he ate the same food, too. Still, it was an adjustment to life. The traffic light changed and Renshaw crossed the street, wondering briefly how many other people chose the same extreme.

There were ten more blocks to his apartment; he was walking up 7th Avenue, his usual route. All of a sudden, the scene of Robertson, alone in his room, reading a book over for the third— fourth?—fifth?—time made him quicken his pace. There would be no further check-ups for Robertson. He was cured, as far as Renshaw was concerned. He had 'made an adjustment', in medical parlance—a rather perfect adjustment, in fact.

Renshaw was seven blocks away from his apartment when he stopped again, standing under the street light to collect a half-forming thought. Then, for the first time in eight years, he crossed over to 8th Avenue and took another route home.

JOAN BAKEWELL

Female Friends

She arrived late, sweeping in. Her mink coat froze the gaze of several shoppers—the effort not to stare cricking their well-creamed but shrivelled necks. It was that kind of shop: cushioned with thick carpet against the shock of its prices. Deidre felt the same twinge as the others, sitting there mouselike at the restaurant table, waiting. Jocasta had made her wait—not vindictively, but in the unspoken confidence that her time was more valuable than Deidre's. It had always been so, a complicit agreement between them ever since their days together at secretarial college. Hadn't Jocasta missed Deidre's 'coming out' because of a theatre date, her engagement party because Mummy had flu and even her wedding because of a tennis final? Yet here, now, was Jocasta turning up, not very late, to Deidre's own modest luncheon invitation. The sudden twinge of female spite died. That's what it meant to have a best friend.

Jocasta didn't have a best friend. She wished she had. She thought of Deidre simply as an old chum, the sort to boost morale and soothe self-doubts about her social standing with her husband's colleagues in the City. On the other hand simply hundreds and hundreds of wonderful people were acquainted with her and a loyal handful wished they knew her better. Once, years ago, Jocasta had hoped her husband himself might grow from a boisterous lover into a best friend. For some reason, puzzling to her, it hadn't happened. He hadn't time to notice for one thing, and to be fair even her intimate conversation stayed with the texture of curtains for the drawing-room and recipes for bouillabaisse. He had learned to listen with one ear. It was to her children she had next looked for such intimacy. Flesh of her flesh, perhaps as they fed at her distended white breasts they would take into themselves something of her that would tip them off to her inner needs. As they grew she spoke to them in forthright terms of love for others, loyalty, integrity, intimacy and eventually sex. The forthright terms on this latter subject tended to be abstract nouns rather than practical verbs. She marvelled as they grew into independent personalities showing no sign of the inner and private sense of emptiness she felt. She took full credit for this blossoming, regarding it as a triumph of maternal influence, which in a way it was. And she spoke sometimes with too noisy a pride about how she had dealt with their sullenness as teenagers, the awkwardnesses of their growing up. Her acquaintances—hundreds of them —plagued by the disagreeableness of their own offspring, listened to Jocasta and marvelled. They never met her children. She was the envy of them all, the self-professing paragon of motherhood they all wanted to be. As Deidre wanted to be. That was why Deidre had asked her to this lunch.

But first there were the social niceties. Jocasta was hard to flatter. 'What, this? My dear, I can't get rid of it—no one will buy it. No, it's no kind of investment. I certainly don't want it any longer. I don't want to wear the skins of all those little animals!' Deidre recalled seeing a protest poster carried aloft by shuffling people in a thin drizzle—'the first owner of your coat died in it'—and she found it odd that Jocasta had now succumbed to their slogan as easily as she succumbed to the one that originally enticed her into the fur salon.

'They were bred for it: that makes it different.'

'Not for me, it doesn't. I honestly wish I could be rid of it.' And she shrugged it from her shoulders with a gesture of disgust that indicated to the shrivelled necks now craning to overhear that Jocasta might be very rich, but she certainly lacked breeding.

They ate well, comparing the merits of different diets as they tucked into smoked salmon with side salad, sipping white wine. They talked about health farms, patchwork cushions, the latest play at the National Theatre. Deidre became talkative as the unaccustomed wine brought pink spots to the centre of her cheeks; then she became confiding. Jocasta, enjoying her trust, perceived that here might be the makings of the friendship that had so eluded her. Deidre might seem a grey creature in Jocasta's gaudy world but she was certainly kind, and fond and attentive. More attentive to Jocasta than her husband or her children had ever been. Jocasta felt a sudden pang of regret. Which is why, when Deidre finally set out her own problem—when Deidre made it clear she wanted advice, Jocasta eschewed her usual flashy answers.

'I can honestly say I would hate, just hate to have a daughter in her teens today. I just don't know what I'd say to her. I simply don't. What can you tell them: "Yes, go ahead, sleep with him"? That's if you even like the boyfriend. Then what happens, what do you do then? What do *they* do then? They quarrel, and she takes up with someone else. Where does it end? It doesn't: she goes from one to another. What's she got to lose after all: the cat's out of the bag. Before you know it, your daughter's a slag and she's not yet taken her "O" levels.'

'Well, actually, Wendy'll only be doing C.S.E.s.'

'I don't think they don't teach them correctly. It has to be that, doesn't it. They know all about the pill and the coil—but not self-respect. These young teachers don't bother with that. What does C.S.E. stand for, anyway?'

Deidre's children went to a comprehensive whose headmistress appeared regularly on *Any Questions?* and all the young teachers were keen on training for parenthood. They had classes in which boys bathed babies and girls painted shelves. Deidre thought it probably only confused them. It certainly confused her. But George had insisted on the school. Things would otherwise be very sticky for him as a Labour councillor. But now Jocasta was about to make everything clear—as good friends did. Deidre ordered crème de menthe for them both with coffee and leant eagerly towards her noticing for the first time the false eyelashes gummed together by generous lumps of mascara.

'Jocasta, what am I to do? Do help me out. You can be such a brick. What did you do about Jackie? You see Wendy's only 15 and she's asking me to let her go to Paris with this boy from the sixth form . . . there'll be four of them. Another pair—so it's bound to mean—well, you know—bed. And Wendy's below the legal age. It isn't even lawful. Do they actually prosecute, d'you know?'

'God knows what's lawful these days. I sometimes think you'd have to do it with a goat in the middle of the rush-hour for anyone to mind.' Silence fell suddenly at the next table; two matrons in Jacqumar scarves looked heavily at each other without blinking. 'Paris will be safe enough I'd say. Gay Paree, after all!'

'But French laws . . . don't the French mind? What about the hotels?' Deidre's supposed whisper raised a neighbouring eyebrow.

'Paris is special, isn't it. They turn a blind eye. Where'd all those writers and painters be without the inspiration of l'amour? They expect it. Remember that weekend we had together after our typing course ended?' Deidre remembered: cherished memories. But had assumed, rightly, it meant nothing to Jocasta.

'Of course, but there weren't any boys with us.'

'Well no, but after all—twin-bedded room and two nubile women—they make films about that sort of thing nowadays.' Jocasta gave a brassy laugh. Deidre had gone suddenly cold, and behind her flushed cheeks she felt pale. She had cared for Jocasta in those days. Not to touch, nothing sensual or wrong. But Jocasta had the same long limbs as Miss Wortley, her adored hockey mistress at Glendower House, and that week in the run-down Paris hotel Deidre had liked to watch her friend undress. Jocasta hadn't noticed at the time. It was only her remark so many years after that brought back that long-forgotten impulse.

Deidre herself had felt a stranger to it long since, what with
George and his established demands, cursory but frequent. Bedrooms were about men and not making too much noise in case
the children heard. How odd, Deidre thought, it had been such a
frail sensation—yet survived in her memory quite keenly.

Jocasta's thoughts had not stayed with Paris. She was gazing
deeply into the dregs of coffee. Deidre was really quite pretty,
nice blonde skin, pale blue made her look washed out but she
certainly wasn't dowdy. And kind, so very kind. Always had
been. Sweet Deidre. If their lives weren't so very different she'd
be a real friend. This appraisal ended, Jocasta commanded
another crème de menthe and leaning forward touched Deidre's
elbows, hunched on the linen cloth, with her long red nails.

'Look, Deidre,' she began slowly—'Let me explain to you
about Jackie. What happened about her. Though I don't know
if it'll . . . well . . . anyway! What happened was this. It was the
week before Christmas and frankly I was in the usual mad panic
. . . dashing here and there! Ian and I were planning a big party.'
She smiled quickly, remembering that Deidre hadn't been invited.
Deidre, not noticing, thought it must be a happy story. 'Jackie,
as you probably know, had a suite of her own at the top of the
house . . . a large bed-sit really but with her own bathroom, of
course, and her own telly. She was 18 after all, entitled to her own
life. She was down from Oxford for the hols, and staying apart
from us quite deliberately, cutting herself off. Ian was furious.
What was so superior about Oxford, he said. He's a Balliol man
himself but Jackie was just at secretarial college. He got quite
impatient with her sullenness, sulking against him in some way,
he thought. But I knew it wasn't. "It's a lover," I thought. "I'm
sure and about time." She'd been so good so far not showing any
interest. And it's just not natural, not to . . . at some point, is it?
Let her ask him round. I said as much to her, in fact. Well, not
directly, not in so many words. But as easily as one can. I indicated—"If you have any special friend, Jackie, do feel you can
invite him. Do invite him. And provided you tidy up your room

you can entertain him upstairs—play records, you know, that
kind of thing. He might like to see your posters!'' God, Deidre,
I nearly said etchings. Etchings! Imagine! Mother to daughter.'
She nudged Deidre's elbow again rather more heavily and her
crimson lips gaped in tinny laughter. 'My mother must be turning
in her grave. We've come so far, haven't we, so far since the
Victorians. We can really take credit for that, Deidre, you and I.
Our generation.'

Jocasta paused, growing suddenly serious again. She began
tracing a line on the white cloth with a scarlet fingernail. Deidre
saw that the varnish was ever so slightly chipped and the fact
pained her. She laid her own hand gently upon Jocasta's as if to
shut the offending blemish from her sight. Jocasta froze: and
ordered a further crème de menthe. The restaurant was emptying
and the waitress made a comment to her colleague as she passed.

'The fact is, Deidre, I came back from shopping late one
afternoon. I'd had the Christmas tree delivered and wanted to
decorate it myself. I've always done it every year. Since I was a
child: it reminds me of Nanny Bunton. So I set up the tub at the
foot of the staircase. Then I needed the decorations. Each year
we put them away in a big box. It's kept for some reason—don't
ask me why—in Jackie's room. Or what was then Jackie's room.'

Deidre began to sense where they story led and folding her
arms sat back in quiet anticipation. She was feeling sleepy from
the syrupy green drinks and quite happy to let Jocasta finish at
her own pace. Yet her imagination raced ahead and pictured in an
instant her own hand turning a strange door handle at the top of
rickety stairs. She started at the forbidden image: Wendy and a
bony youth cavorting on tousled sheets. Deidre leant forward
again the more to sympathise with Jocasta's tale.

'Well, I just breezed into her room, flinging the door wide.
Nothing discreet about me, you know that. And there they were
. . . or rather there was this great heaving and sort of . . . grappling
happening under the bedclothes. With Jackie's head thrown back
on the pillow. And the sound! I was out of the room in a flash.

Quick as a jiffy. But so embarrassed I banged the door. Not
intentionally. Not as disapproval. Just that there was no pretend-
ing I hadn't seen. And that they knew I had.'

Jocasta paused, and Deidre felt a sense of anticlimax . . . no, not
anticlimax. More the sense that in telling a friend, in telling
Deidre, Jocasta had recovered from whatever sense of shock
there had been. And it all seemed so banal. Just a daughter and
her boyfriend. A problem enlightened women like themselves
could come to terms with. All young people did it these days.
And she began to feel almost content that Wendy would be just
like the rest. Jocasta, however, was still scratching the tablecloth
and staring at the scattered crumbs.

'The shock wasn't then, Deidre. It was when they came down.
I heard the noise on the stairs and told myself, "Stay normal,
casual, perfectly relaxed." Me perfectly relaxed! I was shaking I
can tell you. But I'd called out, sort of cheerily—"Tea and
scones, you two . . . in the kitchen!" The point is, Deidre, that
when they came in, it wasn't a boyfriend. It was a girl! I never
slept a wink that night. I tossed and turned. I got all emotional.
I had a really big cry, honestly I did. I couldn't talk to anyone.
Not even to Ian. He'd have hit the roof . . . he might even have
got violent with her. So I had to keep it secret. But he knew
something was upsetting me . . . all that weeping and wailing. In
the end he moved into the spare room. After all, he had work to
do the next day. Finally I took a grip on myself—"Calm down,
calm down, it happens, doesn't it!" ' She paused and looked into
Deidre's eyes as a juicy tear struggled its way through the congealed mascara and across a tired cheek. Her hand flicked it away
vigorously. 'Gay is such a disgusting word for it, don't you think?'

Deidre loved Jocasta. She realised the fact easily and without
surprise, a close womanly love, an embracing soft love. Nothing
more. She was pleased to have been told Jocasta's secret. It was
safe with her. She had captured Jocasta now. The intimacy had
yielded up her own secret.

'No, it's not ugly. If the love isn't ugly. And I'm sure it's not.'

As they left the restaurant and the store, the doorman came forward to call a taxi for Jocasta. She had recovered her composure once again, sailing like a galleon before the wind of Deidre's approval. They would meet again, they said, and not leave it so long. What it was to have a friend, Deidre thought, a friend to love. And for the first time in her life Jocasta felt the same.

BARRY CALLAGHAN

A Drawn Blind

Oldham Beale lived in a yellow brick house with a peaked slate roof. There was an old limestone hitching post half-hidden in the dogwood bushes down along the driveway. Oldham sometimes sat there on a varnished folding chair from his father's sailing sloop. His father had made a small fortune in ball bearings and had spent his money on sailing boats and stone animals carved by a friend in the mortuary business. He'd decorated the front lawn with stone puppies, fawns and lion cubs and inside the house there were brass wind-lamps on the walls and cane deck furniture in the drawing-room. There was a big polished brass bell hanging over the bathtub in the bathroom.

His mother had always kept to herself, cradling two Siamese cats who sometimes in the early morning went out of the house and killed sparrows and left them on the front stoop. She kept scented handkerchiefs in her sleeve and used them to touch her temples while she read romances by Mazo de la Roche, and when her husband drowned in a squall on Lake Scugog, she went out to the garage and got a tyre iron and smashed all the stone animals on the lawn. Oldham, then nearly nineteen, came home and found her sitting on a white wicker stool in the bathroom and she was running boiling hot water into the open tub and the room was dense with steam and she was methodically clanging the brass bell.

Oldham, after he'd entered teacher's college, kept his mother company in the late afternoons and he tried reading aloud the gossip in the newspapers but she had become a secret drinker and her mind wandered as she sat wrapped in a blanket on the veranda, sipping gin from a bone china cup. He'd sit in silence as the sun went down, his long legs stretched out and crossed at the ankles, because there was little more he could say to her. She only cared about Slavs and Jews and their noisy children who were moving on to the street from the South Market.

'Don't you see,' she'd cried one evening, touching her temple with a little white lace handkerchief, 'we're all fakes, like Mazo de la Roche. Did you know her real name was really Mazie Roche. They're overrunning us, those scum, listen to them, and we deserve it, no backbone, any of us.'

Sometimes when the children were playing street hockey she'd call the police and in a little while a yellow patrol car would ease around the corner and a cop would tell the noisy kids to get off the street.

'That's all that's left to count on,' she'd said, 'the police.'

When his mother died he was secure but he kept on teaching history at the Collegiate up on the hill because he liked talking about the mistakes generals made, how history, especially when men were at their most optimistic, was always in decline. In a small book about a courtesan who'd inexplicably committed suicide, he found the epitaph he had carved on his mother's headstone: 'Tired of this eternal buttoning and unbuttoning.' His father's old friend, the mortician, was offended, but he didn't care. He began to collect old books of epitaphs and when he found out that the hill his school was on had been called Gallows Hill because the blue clay had been used to make the bricks for the first death house in the city, he felt a warm confirmation of his sense of how things secretly hung together, and that was really the pleasure he sought in all his books, a confirmation of how he felt about life. He didn't talk to many people and didn't change his mind about many things, and even though the house was filled with all kinds of books, their clutter irritated him, they were in his way. He didn't want to re-read them and yet, because they had been expensive, he couldn't bring himself to give them away or throw them out.

Then one day in a subway station he saw the ticket-taker in the glass cage reading a paperback book, and the man, rather than set the book down and mark his place, would just tear off the cover and then tear off the pages as he finished them, dropping them into a waste can, whittling the book down to nothing. This seemed so sensible to Oldham that from then on he read only paperbacks and even when he sat reading on the front lawn by the old hitching post he placed a little waste can down beside his right shoe.

Then one evening when he was listening to the opening innings of a baseball game, the evening sun filtering through the silver birch trees, the living-room in a lovely rose wash-light, he sat drinking brandy in his rush-bottomed ladderback chair beside the old upright radio and wrote in a neat cramped hand in a book of blank pages bound in black leather. For nearly three months he'd been keeping a journal, not what he did from day to day, but notes and small reflections, and while sitting listening to the broadcast of the ball game and Mudcat Cleever who was pitching a no-hitter, he wrote: 'The deepest root desire we have is to project totally ourselves, cookie-shapes of who we are; hence, Adam's rib becomes Eve so that he can copulate with his image of himself, and the Virgin, she conceives her son out of herself; love thyself as thy neighbour . . .'

He took off his round steel-rimmed glasses and sat with his eyes closed, half-brooding, half-listening. Then, by the seventh innings of the ball game, he was so caught up in Cleever's no-hitter that he suddenly realized he was sitting in total darkness. He wanted to share his excitement because he was on the edge of his chair, hanging on every pitch, but he found himself touched by a bittersweetness and surprise and a flutter of panic because he'd never seen himself as so absolutely alone, and as he stood up he remembered the first time as a boy that he'd been in his father's boat in rough water, and he'd lain down on the deck refusing to look at the waves that smashed broadside and with his eyes shut he'd repeated over and over, 'Jesus Mary and Joseph,' just like he'd heard his mother moaning one late evening alone in the kitchen, but on the boat his father kept calling out, 'Nothing can go wrong, Oldie old kid,' and nothing had gone wrong and Oldham had been ashamed but his father had said, 'You got to feel fear at least once to find out what it is and once you know, then you know how to handle it,' and Oldham, in the dark of his living-room, alone, suddenly smiled, feeling buoyant and unafraid and at ease. He went out for a long walk, forgetting about Cleever and the baseball game.

The more he thought about it the more he liked being alone. He didn't like talking to women for too long and was glad he taught in an all-boys school. Standing by himself in a crowd, or sitting at a bar, his sense of his own aloofness gave him a feeling of security, as if he couldn't be touched, and also a sense of self-discipline. Of an evening, after he'd marked his class papers, and he was a stern marker, he'd go to the movies or a club if there were a good Dixieland band on the stand, and once a week he had supper in the Oak Room in the Edward Hotel, usually milk-fed veal or medallions of beef in wine and mushroom sauce. Then he walked along to the Dindas street strip-joints, watched the show, and hired one of the hookers who lined the lounge walls every night. He liked his no-nonsense approach to the whole matter and though he kept his little notes to himself in his leather-bound book, he was sure too much reflection, too much analysis of the self was a kind of self-hatred, and he was delighted one night when he found a quote, unattributed, in a collection of epitaphs: 'Nowadays not even a suicide kills himself in desperation. Before taking the step he deliberates so long and so carefully that he literally chokes with thought. It is even questionable whether he ought to be called a suicide, since it is really thought which takes his life. He does not die with deliberation, but from deliberation.'

Then late one night there was a soft rain, a falling mist, and

when he went out to sit on the veranda around midnight, the
street lamps glowing up in the caves of leaves in the maple trees
touched him with an almost sensual longing, not for anything
lost in the past, because he had no particular regrets, but it was a
kind of homesickness for the future, a wondering whether in the
midst of his calmness he was already into his decline, and was he
going to end in a fog like his mother or suddenly disappear under
water like his father.

   As he sat with his arms folded across his chest, hugging himself
because he felt an evening chill, he looked at the houses across
the road, thinking they were like a row of crypts in the night and
he began to look up and down the street for lights in the windows,
wondering what went on in all those darkened rooms, because
the big old homes were now rooming houses filled with blacks
and haggard whites.

   He began walking late at night when the streets were empty,
nearly everyone asleep except for a few random lights, and in those
windows the blinds were always drawn, making the light seem
secret and more mysterious. He found himself making up little
scenes, imagining what was going on behind those blinds, as if
he'd walked quickly by an open doorway in one of the down-
town hooker hotels and seen bodies caught in a flash of light and
then they were gone, no names, forgotten, and this left him with
the same feeling as he had sitting down to supper in the Oak
Room, where he was part of the place and yet apart. He didn't
want to meet any of the people who lived in the houses any more
than he would have spoken to people in those rooms in the hotels,
but he liked thinking that there were transient lives being lived
in the half-light of those rooms, lives as mysterious as his own,
because he thought with a sudden rush of satisfaction that if
anyone were to pay any particular attention to him, surely he
would seem a mysterious self-enclosed man to his neighbours.
Certainly motorcycle policemen going by slowly at one and two
in the morning gave him a quizzical look as he sauntered along
the sidewalk in his tweed jacket.

One night, he heard the low, mournful wail of a horn and as he stood listening it sounded like someone playing the Last Post, and so he went out into the street just in time to see a woman in slacks running away through the shadows toward Dupon Street. There was a light in the big front room on the second floor in the house across the street. Someone was pacing back and forth behind the drawn blind. Out on the balcony, a man stood playing a trombone, the horn angled up into the air. A short bald man dressed only in slippers and a dressing gown sidled up to Oldham on the lawn and said, 'Must be up there I bet.'

Oldham said, 'Yes, that's it,' suddenly overcome with the feeling that the man up there with his arms outstretched was reaching out only to him, and that if he only had a horn himself, if only he'd known how to play, he would've stood there on his lawn and blown back at the man outlined against the dark sky, but instead he said over again, 'Yes, that's it.' Then a woman wearing a pink taffeta housecoat and pink pompom slippers joined them, saying, 'Now there's a wacky son-of-a-bitch. You never know what's gonna happen in the night.' The man on the balcony, who was only a shadow in the light from the half-hidden moon, was playing the same mournful notes over and over again, so sonorous that they were chilling, but the bald man began to laugh. Oldham was offended by the laughter.

The police came in a black unmarked patrol car and Oldham stood beside the car waiting while the officers went into the house. Then one of them appeared on the balcony and led the trombone player inside. The car window was open and Oldham could hear the dry rasping voice of the dispatcher over the radio. The woman in pompons who'd come up beside him said, 'Lots of action tonight, someone's always screwing someone.' Then the young policemen came down the walk, smiling, and Oldham said, 'What's the matter?' The cop with the blond razor moustache said, 'Nothing important, guy came home and found his wife in bed with her girlfriend. More of that going on all the time.' They drove away.

Oldham found himself brooding about the police and the horn player and the woman fleeing up the street, and the next day during classes he was distracted and strangely troubled. Two or three times he stood silently nodding his head, and later that night while he was walking he said to himself, 'What'd that dumb dope mean saying it was nothing important.' He felt full of rage and also a sadness for that lonely horn player. A motorcycle cop up ahead was riding half out of his saddle seat, methodically moving along past the row of parked cars. His motor broke the silence with its dry spluttering and Oldham saw that he had a thick stub of chalk in his hand and he was reaching out, swiping at the back wheels, leaving a white slash on the tires. He realized the cop was marking cars, that they'd all get overnight parking tags in the morning, and because the streets around were lined with cars with no place to park he said to himself, 'Why, that's like shooting sitting ducks.'

The next night he carried a damp cloth rolled in a ball in his hand, and he was tense as he walked along on the roadway, dipping down at the back wheel of every car, wiping away the chalk marks. It took him about three-quarters of an hour to cover two blocks. He worked up a sweat. Then he quit because on the other streets he didn't know any of the houses and there were no lights in the windows. They weren't his neighbours.

One week later, later at night, he nodded laconically to a motorcycle cop wearing a white helmet and the cop scowled back at him and the next night he met the same cop on foot. He realized the cop was trying to catch him, and he laughed quietly, but when the cop said, 'You better watch out,' he stepped forward, stern and officious, as if he were dealing with a recalcitrant boy in his classroom, calling into the startled cop's face, 'I beg your pardon,' and the cop took a step sideways with Oldham pursuing him, saying again, even more aggressively, 'I beg your pardon, I beg your pardon.' Then he turned and went back home, leaving the cop alone out in the street.

As he walked up alongside his dogwood bushes, he looked

back at the windows across the street, all of them dark, and he thought how gradually during the week it must have dawned on those people in the morning that there'd been no tickets on their windshields, and what pleased him was that they would have no idea why the tickets had suddenly stopped and they wouldn't know who to ask or even what had gone on. He felt so good as he went into the house that he went upstairs and pulled down the blind in the bathroom window and took off his clothes and got into the tub and took a hot bath. As he stretched out in the soothing water he smiled, knowing that if anyone were standing out in the back in the dark looking up at the light behind his drawn blind they'd have no idea of how secretly satisfied he was.

DAVID PRYCE-JONES

Signatures

Every so often along the road a sign proclaimed the name of another village. These signs were blue, made of enamelled tin, but battered as though habitually pelted with stones. From the car window, little else of the villages could be seen, at most two or three adjoining farm-houses, low out-buildings, barns whose doorways were arched high enough to take a cart loaded with hay. No children, no dogs. Almost forty years ago, conquerors had passed this way—first the Germans going out, then the Red Army coming in. To judge by appearances, it might have happened more recently. This depopulated countryside had the dreariness of an unending grievance.

The road began to twist up past the lower slopes of a pine forest. Morning vapour had been trapped here and there in the moist, receding darkness between the trees. At one point a view of a river below opened in the distance, and then the castle rose ahead like a huge outcrop of grim brownish stone. A sheer glacis wall guarded the approach to the solitary entrance, beyond which were towers and roofs at various angles, and an onion-domed church, more on the scale of a small town. With me I had Marie-Louise's book and her photographs had given the impression of something altogether more domestic.

Beneath the walls was a jumble of houses much in need of paint. Noticing a bar, I parked. The man behind the counter was in conversation with a friend; both were in overalls, both had watery eyes. 'Deutsch,' they repeated loudly, as a plain statement of fact about me. The bottle of schnapps standing between them had no label. The man behind the counter refilled their glasses, and pushed a third one over to me. In German I asked for something to eat for breakfast, and whether there was coffee instead of schnapps, but the resources of language between us had been exhausted. The men stared for a while, then turned back to each other. Outside an elderly woman walked by, her back and shoulders bowed under the bundle of firewood she was carrying. The knot of her headscarf hung beneath her chin. She did not glance sideways in at the bar.

Traffic could apparently drive in and out through the castle gateway, but I preferred to enter on foot. The steepness of the climb soon left me out of breath. Many more small houses were crowded within the fortifications. I had the sense of some busy life too secret to reveal itself. A one-storey building, deserted now, suggested former alms houses. In one of the towers of the enclosing walls someone was rearing poultry; planks and bits of old timber were sticking out of the open casements of another. The road finally widened and turned into a courtyard, dominated by the central block and the two wings of the house. This was the façade which I recognised from Marie-Louise's photographs, this was the eighteenth-century aspect which she had emphasised— one could scarcely believe that something so classical would be squeezed within medieval precincts. Part of the rather formal double staircase up to the main door had been boarded over, and before it stood a local tourist bus, empty. An arrow, painted black on a strip of plywood tacked to the stonework of a balustrade, indicated a ticket office. It was shut. I rang the bell. The stout woman who eventually arrived was wearing a man's leather boots, she was wiping the palms of her hands down her apron. She too had a headscarf tied around her head. From what she seemed to be telling me, and from the way she pointed at the bus, I deduced that individual visits were not allowed, and that special prior arrangements had to be made for groups through the state tourist agency.

She looked old enough to have known Marie-Louise and Leo, perhaps even to have worked for them before the war, so I mentioned their names. Fingers outstretched with the surprise of it, she gestured that I ought to wait. So I perched beside a statue which had lost its arms and head. Its pair had once stood at the other side of the courtyard, but only pieces of the pedestal remained. I remembered Marie-Louise's account of how she and Leo had bought statues in Venice during their honeymoon, how the gondola transporting them had somehow tipped over under the weight, and with what absurd difficulties the statues had been recovered. Instead of a tourist bus, on that very spot every single day there used to be a dozen landaus, each with a liveried coachman and groom, for the convenience of guests, and around the spokes of the wheels flowers were always woven—no other details of their visits here seemed to have impressed my parents quite so unforgettably. The fading outlines in red and black of a sundial could still be made out above the main door. Patches of plasterwork had fallen away between the windows. There were leprous stains, broken drainpipes and gutters. The fittings for windowboxes had rusted.

Flowers had always been Marie-Louise's hallmark. There was said to have been several acres of hot-houses on the estate here. When I had first been taken to meet her, she was living near London in a cottage put at her disposal by a friend. It was a time of post-war austerity and perhaps I was unduly impressionable but I had never seen anything to equal the extravagance of her flowers. People like my parents provided her with clothes and food and little luxuries, to be sure, but all her visitors knew that the way to her heart was through the present of a gardenia, hyacinths, poinsettias, something in a pot or a bowl to last. Even when she became ill, and virtually dependent on charity, she never cut back on flowers. After her death, when we all had to cope, we were amazed by the number of florists and nursery gardens where she had opened accounts, and the size of the sums owing.

And books too. Her reading glasses had diamanté frames which seemed out of character, for there was nothing the least vulgar in her knack of discerning good new books. She ordered them recklessly from Paris, Rome, New York, and expected everyone to be able to discuss them with her. In her time this castle had been filled with writers, musicians, artists, the famous and the spongers alike, put up for as long as they wished in the towers or elsewhere, and left to the business of being or becoming celebrities. How many of them had arranged to be photographed showing off in one of the landaus? Not that Marie-Louise was a snob. She was kept amused by what she called 'the racket'. Doing as she pleased happened to tie up with spontaneous generosity—that her fortune was limitless in those days was quite beside the point. She expected nothing of all those guests, and she was right about that too, for when she was no longer a princess but a down-and-out émigré, many of them could not even take the trouble to answer letters, or send her a bouquet at Christmas. Pinning her down at that stage to the business of keeping within a budget, as her friends had to acknowledge, a little ruefully, was simply fatuous. She made out that it was all rather funny, twisting a Cinderella-in-reverse fairy-tale out of her life. Except when her publishers insisted on cutting out of her memoirs several stories, including one about how a French novelist, then at the height of his world-wide reputation as a progressive, not to mention a personal friend of Stalin's, had stolen one of the Renaissance miniatures from her collection. Quite unable to grasp why she could not tell the truth, and nothing but the truth, for once she became furious.

But then her sense of possession was generally vague. Towards the end she had frequently used friends' accounts and signed their names too, for anything expensive which she particularly wanted. She shop-lifted as well, and if asked, would talk about it as though she had been doing hardly more than making stylish claims on things which were somehow hers by right. My parents had neither confirmed nor denied rumours that whenever she had been caught the shopkeepers never felt like prosecuting, as soon as it was explained to them who she was and how rich she had been. Perhaps they shared my impression that neither her fortune nor its loss had mattered enough to affect her. Her memoirs did make her some money, of course, and otherwise she had kept going by selling off one by one her Matisse drawings, several of them presented to her by the artist himself, when she had owned a house in Paris during the mid-Twenties. According to some people, she had jewels in reserve, but if so, none were found when finally we had to open a fund and solicit contributions to pay off her debts.

Leo, whom I had never known, remained rather lost in the background. A remote or lazy man, he appeared to have been easily pleased, condescending to everyone and everything. He had concentrated on his race-horses, his shooting and his mistresses, the last of whom had lent him indefinitely her house in Miami, where he had died as much of boredom as of anything specific. In her book Marie-Louise comments somewhere that she and Leo had been obliged to accommodate to a society in which lovers were the evidence of being attractive—'only the poor and the ugly remained faithful.' So they had even made a grace of drifting. This castle had been handed down through generations of his family to Leo, and it ought to have signified security, but when I looked round at Leo's natural setting I had an almost physical sensation of the pre-war restlessness of the place, its indulgences, the balls and weekends and theatre parties, the comings and goings between Budapest and Vienna and Prague always under the mounting storm.

The woman returned. She was accompanied by a youngish man in a German *loden* overcoat, loose-fitting but which gave him a certain distinction. If his face was oddly long and thin, it was because his eyes were set so close together, so narrowly. The bridge of his nose must have been uncomfortably in his vision. He drew himself up straight and for a moment I thought he might click his heels.

He said, 'Sie sind Deutsch.'

'Nein, Englisch.'

'Ach so. Aber Sie kommen auf Besuch.' Was some extra muscular tension apparent behind the bony cheeks? He was the resident curator, he explained, there was an authorised group already visiting the gardens, but instead of joining them he would make an exception and show me personally round the castle. I was a curator myself, or specially interested in culture and history? No? Then perhaps a relation of the former owners? How otherwise did I know their names?

I did not feel like giving away more information than I had to, so ventured, 'You know the princess's book?'

He nodded. 'I should like to have it. For the house, of course.'

My copy, now on the seat of my car, had a dedication in Marie-Louise's generous hand. I said nothing, worrying as always in those unequal circumstances, about the impossibility of either giving or withholding any gift.

According to his lights, he did his best I suppose. At least I think he believed what he was repeating about the castle as a function of feudal society, and later as a stronghold in the Thirty Years War, when religious passions, if I understood his pedantic German correctly, really had been no more than class-expressions. First we walked down a corridor into the main hall. Tapestries had once been framed there in ornate plaster cartouches, bare now.

'The Soviets liberated the Gobelins,' he said without the least irony. 'It is not known for certain where they are now.'

'Liberated?' I could not help myself.

'The former owners had no right to them,' he said. 'Or to anything else for that matter, since they produced nothing.'

Scaffolding was up behind the shuttered main door—no sign, however, of any work in progress. There was an airless smell. The main reception rooms were saddening, full of Second Empire or fake French furniture in dusty silks, pictures varnished brown and some of the canvases holed or ripped, a few late Chinese objects and lacquered screens. On the ceilings were fittings from which chandeliers had been wrenched off.

'You see how luxuriously they used to live here,' he said. 'They amassed these things at our expense, before the People's Republic. I am cataloguing the Old Masters.'

I was about to ask whether the pictures could be restored too, but judged it more prudent to keep quiet.

From the hall he led the way into the far wing, and so to the private theatre, once one of the more famous rooms in Europe— the Empress Maria Theresa and Goethe and Napoleon had all in their day seen performances staged there. Marie-Louise had been very proud of it, and had fully illustrated it in her book. Though stripped of its period seats, it was otherwise more or less unspoilt. Painted plaster giants supported the carved proscenium arch. On the walls were frescoes of Columbine and Harlequin Pierrot, zanies, performing monkeys, dancers and clowns and courtiers, with *trompe l'oeil* trophies, though some of them were real by way of further joking, and trick glass and mirrors placed to catch one's own sudden reflection—one rococo fantasy after another. It had been worthwhile to come here just for this.

'Sehen Sie da,' the curator was pointing to a *fête champêtre* scene, in which harvesting peasants, bottles up-ended in their mouths and their clothes in some disorder, were lolling together in golden fields. 'That is what the aristocracy thought of agricultural labourers. Only fit to be drunks and boors.'

I took him up. 'Look harder, and you'll see that the lords and ladies are part of the fun too. Everyone is sharing in the normal human delight at bringing in the harvest. There's no criticism anywhere in that painting. It's a pastoral, not a debauch—and,' I added, dropping my guard, 'for the first time here I can recognise something of the spirit of Princess Marie-Louise.'

'Forty gardeners worked here until the war. I know, because my father was one. They treated us like that. They despised us. We had nothing.'

'If that's so, then things haven't changed,' I replied. 'When I wanted breakfast down in the town, I was offered schnapps by a couple who were much drunker than any of the peasants in your fresco. And there was an old woman lugging sticks on her back as her forebears have always been doing, it hasn't helped her that the castle is in different hands.'

He was about to raise his voice at me, but stopped himself. I understood that I was not worth a quarrel to him. Instead he led me straight back past the scaffolding in the main hall, but paused on the way out at his office. Originally this must have been a little reading-room, possibly Leo's study. Apparently it had not been looted. A *toile de Jouy* covered the walls, and matched the curtains. A Biedermeier writing desk of rosewood with ebony inlay was obviously the curator's now, while above it hung a life-size portrait of a labrador, named as 'Boy' on the frame's tablet. Behind the glass of a bookcase I spotted what had perhaps been Marie-Louise's presentation copies of Gide, Romain Rolland, Marthe Bibesco, Gerhard Hauptmann, Karel Capek, Bunin.

The visitor's book was opened for me to sign. Its hand-made paper was of a quality unfindable today; the leather-bound cover had a coronet embossed at the centre. I turned over the pages. Remarkable how between the wars people, Germans and Austrians especially, wrote their names as if unable to master a pen-nib, pushing it up and down in illegible strokes. Princess Olga of Greece had a page all to herself, as did the Salzburg Festival personalities of Reinhardt, von Hofmannsthal and Richard Strauss. And there, for Christmas 1936, were the signatures of my parents. My mother had written several sentences as well, beginning, 'Comme nous avons été heureux ici avec vous . . .' Had I been here before, then, for that first Christmas of my life? And if not, where had they left me, and why?

'Please, sign,' said the man edging up to me. His *loden* had an outdoor masculine smell, and I had a sudden impression of him with a rifle out after stags in the pine forest. He glanced at his watch to hurry me on.

'I shan't,' I said. 'The owners of this house wouldn't have liked

me to sign unless they had invited me here themselves. I'm not
your guest.'

'You think I haven't received people like you before? They all
sign, I assure you. The former owners thought no more of you
than they did of us. You think I don't know?'

Until that point I had pitied him in his ignorance and his
prejudices. The courage to be oneself would mean nothing to him,
poor man. His definition of happiness could have no room in it
for that visitor's book and what it stood for. It came to me how
Marie-Louise had suffered in the end, in the dead of an English
winter, in a hospital room so filled with mimosa that the effect
was more macabre than cheerful. Still I had never heard her
complain.

'Their only skill was in making claims on you,' he was shouting
now, 'and they were not any richer because others were poor on
their behalf.'

I laid down the pen and shut the book and was about to explain
a little better, when I looked up and in those singularly close
compressed eyes caught something unknown to me, something
yellowish and flaring, which animal instinct at once warned me
was hate its purest.

ELIZABETH TROOP

Daddy's Girl

It was a holiday of desperation and convenience, although neither of them would have admitted it. They were two work-mates who did not get on: Sheila from Ruislip, with a gap in her front teeth and naturally blonde, silky hair that made her look like a Yorkshire terrier, and Joy—dark and intense—from Liver-pool. Joy was recovering from what, in the office, had been called 'flu', which seemed to have left her with marks on her wrists. August had come and gone, typists had come and gone, like migrating birds, to the Greek Islands and Torremolinos. Older secretaries flashed their snaps of Keswick and Loch Lomond. Mr Dootson, it was said, had drifted along French canals with a lady not his wife. But Sheila and Joy had not gone away at all.

Sheila, plump and noisy, chattered about her plight in the office. She usually went away with her parents, but this year had felt she was really too adult to accompany them to the Felpham bungalow; she had gone there since she was a small girl in white cotton ankle socks and Clark's sandals. Daddy was alarmed; he saw her defection as a sign of future loss. His little girl would sever her life from his. She knew he sensed this, worried for him. She worried about him in any case—he still rushed to her room when she had nightmares (which she still did) and comforted her in a way she was beginning to find disturbing. Yet she could tell no one. Daddy's face had crumpled like one of Mummy's soufflés when she had tried to talk to him about it. He had gone bright red, and left to prune the roses.

'What are you going to do for a holiday then, pet?' he would enquire, puffing on his pipe. He and her mother had come back, wind-reddened, weeks before. Sheila said a girl from the office wanted to go away with her for a fortnight. It was a lie—she was reading the travel stuff in the colour supplement when he asked —now she would have to go on from there and do it. He would never let it rest. The trouble was, most people had been away, except Joy. She knew what Joy thought of her; it was apparent, Joy looked at her the way a lot of girls did; she was liked well enough, but it was considered odd that she still lived at home and seemed much younger than her age. She was twenty-nine.

Joy, marooned in her bed-sitter since her lover went back to his wife, had decided not to go away that year. The physical and spiritual hangover from her messy attempt to go on the final trip (she had slashed her wrists half-heartedly, and then rung for an ambulance) had made her aggressive and then full of distorted rage. She had decided to re-plan her life; had signed up for a series of philosophy lectures to carry her through the autumn evenings, had given up on the receding summer. She had made a duty visit to her china-doll mother in Suffolk, lasting out only two days of what was intended to be a long weekend. Her mother, always unobservant, had said she never looked so bonny or relaxed. She left the chintz and the cosy chats, and returned to grey Camden.

Over a plastic cup of tea in the canteen, Sheila plucked up her courage to ask Joy if she had ever thought of going to Guernsey. Joy, whose fantasies ran more to a voyage up the Nile, or a trek across trans-Siberia, shook her head. She asked if it was cheap, just to make conversation.

'Very,' said Sheila. 'Especially now, at the end of the season. The crowds have gone, the bays are beautiful, apparently.' She waited.

Out of lethargy, and a sort of fatalistic rude gesture to the world at large, Joy agreed to go. It seemed to her a grim joke; it

was the most ludicrous thing she could contemplate, so far
removed was it from any wish or desire she'd ever had.

'I don't know what they will do, with both of us away, though,'
Sheila fretted. Joy looked at her in amazement. They were both
totally dispensable, all they did was file the odd document and
invoice, and help out with the typing. It was a University Publishing House, and Joy had stayed only because she had been concen-
trating on her personal rather than her professional life. The pay
was adequate, the job undemanding; it left her time to dream of
the future, when he was to divorce his wife and marry her. It was
plush, warm, a womb away from the harsh realities. Index-linked
pension scheme, three weeks' holiday . . . Sheila had worked there
from leaving school. One of Daddy's friends was in the accounts
department.

Joy decided she would use Guernsey as a watershed between
her old life and her new. It would mark the end of the life of
illusion, of waiting. Once back she would be dynamic, pragmatic,
ordinary, *changed*.

Even before they embarked on the ferry at Southampton she
was bored. They had eaten three dubious snack bar meals,
waiting for the time when they could get on to the boat. Sheila
was apologetic—she had messed up the times, she said. Once they
were on, Joy tried to avoid her. The afternoon had been almost
too much—how was she going to spend two weeks with the girl?

Sheila found her staring at the wake of the boat, seagulls
screaming for the garbage floating after them.

'We get in at five. I didn't tell you, but the crossing is supposed
to be awful just at the end. Rocks, you know. Can I get you
anything? You're not feeling sick?'

'No, just unsociable.' Sheila picked up the awful orange rucksack she had brought and got out a Cox's orange pippin. She
plunged her gappy teeth into it. Joy turned and walked away,
down to the bar. To think she might have holidayed with him, if
she hadn't given him that silly ultimatum. Then it might have
been the South of France, he was fond of Eze, he told her—a little

village perched above the blue-green Med. Not this farcical
blustery voyage to somewhere she did not want to go. Sheila was
togged up like a camper, in hearty shoes, slacks, a reefer jacket
and worst of all, a little bobble hat made of wool.

'I thought we were staying in an hotel,' she had ventured to
say.

'Oh,' said Sheila, blushing. 'This is just for the voyage. I have
more formal things in my rucksack. In case there are cocktail
parties, or the odd dance.' Joy shuddered. It was like journeying
with a fluffy Persian kitten, when one desired tigers.

A skinful of lager, and Joy felt slightly better. They had chosen
their reclining seats, and Sheila had washed and put some Oil of
Ulay on her round, pale cheeks. Joy almost expected her to get
out curlers and put on a frilly nightdress. She took a tartan rug
out of her case and said to Sheila that she thought she would go
on deck for a while.

'You are coming back, though?' asked the girl. Joy felt mean.
She was, after all, quite sweet. Though annoying.

'Of course. It's just that I like to feel the elements a bit.'

'Rather you than me.'

Sheila took out her Catherine Cookson paperback and began
to read, for all the world as if she was at home in bed in Ruislip.

The elements were wild. Joy pushed her spray-spattered face
against the force of the gale. The deck lurched violently, up and
down, first one way then the other. There was no one else out
there. She felt exhilarated, as if the salt water was eating into her
grey, dirty soul. She wondered how Daddy's girl was coping,
downstairs, but she brushed the thought away. She was not,
after all, her sister's keeper.

When she went down eventually she found moaning prostrate
bodies, and an aroma of vomit. Some rushed past her to the
nearest cloakroom. She looked for Sheila. Empty cola tins and
sandwich wrappers floated among dead cigarette ends. Sheila
was not one of the victims. She was sitting, placid as ever, cuddling
a fat baby, who also smelled of sick.

'Madonna and child—what a picture.' Joy had to smile. 'What are you doing?'

'Helping out. The poor mother is feeling lousy, and she has two more little ones. They are all in the loo.' Her moon face beamed. She patted the baby on the back.

'I wouldn't do that if I were you,' said Joy. Suddenly she could not stand the moans and the smell. 'I'm going back up on deck. See you when we dock.'

She felt a little queasy herself now, having been prompted by so much nausea down below. But the astonishment she felt at seeing Sheila coping was enough to steady her. Of course, there was nothing so marvellous about *coping*.

She rocked with the boat's rhythm, up and down, up and down. Gradually it steadied, and became calmer. She was thrilled by the mass of the sea, dark and wild. It was at times like these that she felt it would have been great to be male. It conjured up prospects of being Conrad, or Malcolm Lowry, of making the escape from the land—of the tough life, the life of a loner. We are just bloody bags of entrails, she thought, not allowed to become pure mind, pure intellect. It was the main difference between the sexes, and one that never changed, no matter how much of a feminist one was.

As if to mock at her and echo her thought, the dull ache in her side began, reminding her that her own female processes were about to start their lunar activity. She took out *Heart of Darkness* from her coat pocket, and by the light of a torch, began to read.

At dawn she went down, to find Sheila in the queue for coffee, chatting to two male students, all spots, badges and burgeoning beards.

'Come and meet Tony and Rick. Tony is reading French at Warwick. I don't know what Rick is studying.' Sheila giggled. Joy sighed.

'Hi,' said the students, in unison. 'Can I get you something—toast? A sausage?' The fair one had asked, while the other rattled the cash in his jeans pocket.

'Just coffee, I never eat breakfast. And I'll get it myself,' Joy
said. How could Sheila be so stupid, chatting up two louts like
this. They might even be staying in St Peter Port, they might
become a nuisance. She stared at her reflection in the large urn.
She looked alarmed, untidy, as ghastly as they did; she had read
until three, and it was only five a.m. now. People were lying
around in abandoned sleeping positions. The aroma of sea-
sickness still wafted over the boat. Only Sheila looked as bright
as a button. She had even put on pink lipstick, and dusted her
face with compressed powder.

'Who's your intellectual friend, then?' said Rick, pulling out the
Penguin Conrad from Joy's pocket.

'Oh, don't be so *childish*,' Joy snapped taking the book from
his hand, going over and sitting by the Duty Free Shop.

'Don't take any notice. She is always snappy,' she heard Sheila
say. The three of them went over to the opposite corner where
there was a slot machine. Tony played this, and the sound of the
clicks and whirrs mingled with the giggles from Sheila and Rick.
Joy thought suddenly of Roger, his striped shirts and grey suits,
his dislike of what he called the plebeians. He would laugh at the
whole scene. No, that wasn't true; he wouldn't be there. He
never exposed himself to any kind of harassment of this sort;
his was the world of scheduled flights, luxury hotels and private
beaches. Which perhaps explained why he was not with her. She
rose, and went over to the others.

Sheila gave the lads the name of their hotel, which Joy thought
rather a mistake. Still, the students went off to their boarding
house with just a casual wave of the arm, and a dropped remark
about seeing them around the port, perhaps.

'*Perhaps*,' said Sheila, looking mournful. 'That means they are
going to look around for better talent.'

'Oh, I'm sure it doesn't,' said Joy. 'They seemed nice, genuine
fellows. You were getting along well with them.' Until I came
along, she thought. Poor Sheila, she needed a holiday romance.
'I'll keep out of your way, if you want to see them,' she added.

'Didn't you like them? Tony said you looked very bright. He's the one doing French. But you were so snooty.'

'Sorry.'

They found they were not in the main body of the hotel, but in the annexe. Joy was quite pleased, it meant that the boys would probably not find them, if they looked them up. Sheila was disappointed; she said of course it didn't matter to Joy, as she had obviously stayed in posh hotels, but she hadn't.

'I'm sure your boyfriend, the one who used to pick you up in the Jaguar, took you to four-star hotels.'

'No,' said Joy. 'He used to take his wife.'

'Oh, sorry,' said Sheila. They unpacked. There really wasn't much to talk about now that they were stuck together in a double room. Sheila, having unpacked her cocktail and dance dress and hung them in the cupboard, put her separates into the chest of drawers. Bending to open the bedside table cupboard, to put in her beauty preparations, she screamed.

'What is it now?' Joy was lying in her bed, reading a guide they had been given at the hotel desk.

'It's too awful. Look . . .'

In the little cupboard was a full chamber-pot.

'Just leave it,' said Joy. 'It means they've forgotten it. They'll empty it tomorrow.'

'Ugh. How do you know? They might just leave it.'

'Then you do it.' Joy stubbed out her cigarette. 'Come on, let's go over to lunch. Forget it.'

The lunch was excellent, fish soup, veal escalope, fresh vegetables and lovely ice cream. Joy felt the holiday might not be so bad. Sheila was still fretting about the chamber-pot.

The first few days passed. The chamber-pot remained in the cupboard, Sheila never mentioned it, and Joy looked when she was out of the room. They walked, after Sheila's initial objections. They had a pact that they would play it cool if they saw the boys again, although Joy could tell that Sheila would not be able to resist a date. One afternoon there was a commotion at the harbour. A small boy had fallen off the tower at the end of the jetty, and they were searching for his body. Joy was moved by this. It seemed to her tragic that a child had gone into that grey sea, so silently. She remembered her own silly attempt to cause attention, that Sunday in the bathroom. Sheila was upset too, and said, typically, that she was going to *spend*.

'It is the only thing to do, when you feel sad,' she said. Joy didn't want to accompany her; she said she would go and read in a quiet spot, and meet Sheila back at the hotel.

A shadow fell over her book. She looked up to find Tony standing there.

'What was all the fuss in the harbour, earlier?' he asked, squatting beside her.

'A boy was drowned.'

'Sad.' He stretched out, full length beside her. 'And how do you like this place?'

'Not bad. The food is good. I like the port, it is sweet . . .'

'And your unsuitable friend, she is enjoying it?'

Joy had to laugh.

'No, not too much. She would enjoy it more if she'd found a holiday romance.'

'But not you?'

'That's the last thing I want.'

'She's quite sweet, Sheila.'

'If you like the type.'

He didn't say if he did or did not. She went on reading, and eventually he got up and began to walk off.

That night the two of them were in the pub that Sheila and Joy used quite often. Rick seemed very edgy.

'He had a breakdown, left Warwick last term. Be nice to him,' said Tony, squeezing Sheila's arm, while Rick went for the drinks.

'But not *too* nice,' said Joy.

'Not drugs, was it?' Sheila asked. Daddy would never approve of her consorting with junkies.

'No. Overwork. Ssh.' Rick put down the lager and the gin and orange for Sheila. Joy hadn't thought girls still drank gin and orange. They had a reasonable enough time—Joy thought Sheila chattered rather too much and several times had hovered on the edge of asking Rick how he felt, but she and Tony had managed to salvage the situation.

'I think we should split up,' said Sheila, that night, when they lay in their twin beds. Turning towards Joy she revealed she was crying. 'I think they both like you best. Which one do you want?'

'I don't want either.'

Sheila turned her face to the wall.

Sheila was as good as her word. She dressed early, and break-fasted, and Joy didn't see her for the rest of the day. When she got back in the evening for dinner, her hair was Afro-ed and she was wearing a smart French T-shirt and jeans.

'I decided to do something about myself,' she said. 'I'm sick of being Daddy's girl.'

'Good for you,' said Joy.

'You should buy some new gear,' said Sheila. 'You dress like a man.' It was true. Joy surveyed her blue battered Jean Machine coat and her beige cords. But she couldn't bring herself to change.

'At least in my bikini you know I am female,' she said. 'Even if I am not as voluptuous as you.' Sheila laughed. Joy felt like emptying the chamber-pot over her silly head.

The second week began with some bad weather. Joy would put a mac over her bikini and head for a secluded bay, away from the trio. Sheila seemed to be leading them both on: she came back late at night when Joy was tucked up with Joseph Conrad. Usually she was what she called 'squiffy'.

'Do you think Daddy would approve of all this?' Joy asked one night.

'Daddy can get stuffed.' Sheila didn't bother to use the Oil of Ulay anymore, but sank into drunken slumber with face made up and clothes on.

Tony appeared, as he had that first time, while she was scribbling a letter to her mother. He sat down and rubbed his hand along the length of her leg.

'Don't do that,' she snapped. Actually it felt rather nice.

'Don't you want some of what Sheila is getting?' he asked.

'I certainly do not.'

He laughed, but she could see he wasn't pleased.

'She's twice the woman you are,' he said.

'Then she can have twice the fun,' she said, opening her book again. He still stayed, which surprised her, opening up a book of poems in French and intoning them quietly to himself. It was very annoying.

'*Si vous n'avez rien à me dire—Pourquoi venir auprès de moi?*'

What did that mean, she wondered. Her schoolgirl French was poor. 'If you have nothing to say to me, why do you come near to me' was the best she could do. There was a picture of Victor Hugo on the cover of the book.

'He lived here in exile,' said Tony, noticing she was interested. 'He was great. I really like him. Tough—a real old tough guy. He used to seduce all the maids, up there, in his house, and walk the town. His wife and youngest daughter were miserable here. They went back to Paris, and his wife wrote that Adèle, that was his youngest daughter, was miserable, and he said "I'll dedicate a poem to her . . ." Isn't that a fantastic remark?'

'Quite,' she said. It was, actually.

'His eldest daughter, Léopoldine, drowned, just after she was married. Very sad—he really never got over that.'

She looked at him with more interest, not having expected such tenderness, under the flip male attitudes. *Léopoldine*. It was a lovely name.

Tony pulled out a bottle of wine and a corkscrew from his bag. She was slightly annoyed—it meant he had planned this little assault. What the hell—she had no reason not to have a brief fling. He wasn't too bad; it might mean she would rejoin the human race. He had one paper cup with him. So, it wasn't planned. She was slightly disappointed. He handed her the full cup, and drank from the bottle himself.

'Are you going to teach French, when you get your degree?' She felt formal, she had shrunk a little since she knew he was not planning any seduction.

'I haven't thought about it. I can't see that far ahead. I would like to work somewhere abroad. It's dead, England, don't you feel that?'

'I thought it was just me.' She shivered.

'Rick is an interesting type,' he said. 'Rick nearly blew his mind, drugs, drink, everything. He hates university. Your friend is doing him some good—she's so—simple. We tossed for her, you know, but I fixed it so that Rick won. She's a hot little number.'

'And I just thought she was a Daddy's girl.' Joy felt depressed. At least Sheila was doing somebody some good. 'I thought you both er . . . were . . .'

'No,' he said, quickly. 'I always fancied you. It's a bit late now, though—I mean, we can't start anything on the last couple of days. Can we?'

'I don't see why not,' she said.

She put down the paper cup and stretched out. 'We can try.'

It didn't work. It had been forced, cold. He zipped up his jeans, and then knelt and hugged her as if she was a child.

'My fault,' he said. 'Sorry.' She turned over, face against the sand, and he covered her with her tartan rug as if she was a corpse. She heard him trudge away.

Surprisingly, because her body had in a way responded to the sexual mechanics, she was relaxed enough to sleep, and did. When she woke it was greyer and colder than it had been. She pulled on her Breton striped jersey and her jeans, over her bikini.

She walked along, kicking sand with her bare foot. There was only one other person walking, an old man with a white beard and a long black overcoat; one of the strange sorts you found in sea places—an eccentric painter type, perhaps. She, going faster, passed him. He tipped his large black hat at her and said '*Bonjour*'. Funny, the mixture of French and English here; it was like a watered-down version of France.

When she got back Sheila was lying on the other twin bed, her face encased in a beauty mask. Her eyes were intensified, like a clown's, and they followed Joy as she marched about, shoving clothes into drawers, rinsing out her bikini, sluicing cold water on her face.

'You seem angry. Are you coming to the hotel dance tonight?' Sheila spoke oddly, her lips were congealed by the rigours of the facial mask.

'No. And I'm not angry. I just—' She was going to say she had a wonderful sexual experience on the beach, but she decided against it. 'I just feel tired. I walked on the beach. I saw this strange old man—long overcoat, black hat. Weird.'

'Oh, I know him. I've often seen him. His name is Victor something. Hugo.'

'Don't be daft.'

'He told me his name, and he said something else funny. Your French is probably better than mine. Something like, "*Tu ressembles à Léopoldine*." What do you think it means?'

'It means "You are like Leopoldine." ' Joy stared at her. 'He can't have said that. He just *can't*.'

'He's probably a looney,' said Sheila. 'Some poor old soul.'

Joy stared at the white cracked moon of Sheila's face. It wasn't fair, it really was not fair. Her rage against the whole vast complicity of life rose in her like nausea. She could do nothing, nothing about it. This doll on the bed did not even know what she was doing. Perhaps that was the secret, not to *know*. Not to want. Not to desire something other. With deliberate movements she approached the bed.

'What have I said? You look so odd . . .' Joy bent and opened the tiny bedside cupboard, at once despairing and yet full of a strange wild humour. The chamber-pot was still in there, still full. With great force she threw it over the prone girl. The yellow liquid dripped down the white mask. Sheila's frightened eyes looked out at her, sorrowful, betrayed.

'You are quite mad. I am sorry for you,' said the tiny voice of Daddy's girl.

J. E. HINDER

And Far from Home

As far as the eye could see the desert was empty except for a heap of stones topped by a wooden cross of the German variety. And the wireless-truck.

Under its sun-bleached camouflage-net, the truck squatted beneath the blazing sun, surrounded by petrol-cans, water-containers, kitbags, smoke-blackened tins, a German ammunition-box, blankets, a charging-engine and one chair, crimson-silk upholstered with gilt legs. It was early afternoon, 23 October, 1942, and on the bonnet of the vehicle the popular egg-frying demonstration might well have been performed. But there were no eggs.

Driver-Mechanic Sheepridge poured his shaving-water into the radiator and peered impassively at the sleeping figure beneath the mosquito-net.

'He's supped three parts of the sodding bottle, Art,' he remarked, 'so you'll not wake him until he's right.'

Lance-Corporal Topson smiled vaguely.

'Johnny Walker,' he murmured.

'Johnny what!' said Sheepridge. 'Not fit for a bloody camel. Bottled in Alex. Not a drop sold till it's one day old. He'll wake when he's right. I'm going to brew up, anyways.' He poured petrol into a sooty oleomargarine tin and with a careless flourish, dropped a match in it.

As he slept, Sergeant Crompton found himself once more in that city of his dreams that was Cairo and yet not quite Cairo.

'*Thank you George,*' *said the painted girl at the table as the waiter brought the coloured water. Her face cracked in a wide grin, exposing uneven metal teeth. A drunken Argyle and Sutherland Highlander attempted a solo dance to the terrible band as it echoed through the bare grubby cabaret. Crompton stared unsmiling at the woman and her face instantly changed to that of Yaffa, the Palestinian ATS Corporal, Yaffa, that Rose of Sharon among all those bearded lady-wrestlers, Yaffa, dropped in his path like manna by some local deity.*

The surroundings had changed, of course. They were in Lady Russell's club in the Sharia Maaraouf, with iced drinks and profiteroles and M. Poliakin on stage performing his popular trick of playing the bow with the violin. Paganini. Crompton found himself explaining to Yaffa how truly innocent was his relationship with the incredibly exotic Greek girl who sold the tickets at the Diana Cinema. But Yaffa, ignoring explanations, M. Poliakin and the profiteroles, rose and stormed out, taking with her the fabric of the vision and leaving him on a tram of the Cairo Electric Railway and Heliopolis Oases Company.

Here he sat opposite an ancient person whose bandaged foot had swelled to three times normal size and from which there leaked a Chartreuse fluid embedded with complaining flies. A passenger with a tube in his neck just beneath the Adam's apple was pointing to his affliction in frenzied vindication of a demand to be carried free. In vain: piercingly the conductor blew his whistle, the tram stopped and the driver began to assault the passenger with a bamboo cane. A smell of decaying meat, olive-oil drains and lilac overpowered the dreaming Crompton and a damp, reddish dusk descended. A wet sandstorm? Not in Cairo, surely.

'He'll have to wake up soon, eh, Percy?' said Topson. His costume was simple: the remnants of a pair of canvas shoes tied to his feet with aerial-wire and a pair of dirty drawers (cellular). 'We could be moving.'

'We shall be moving,' grunted Sheepridge, writing grimly on a lined pad. 'Today's the day.'

Topson shrugged and gazed dreamily across the wasteland. A hawk hovered, motionless, in the blue sky.

'Make yourself useful and fry up some bacon,' said Sheepridge.

'There's ten tins in the back I whipped from the stores at Amirya.' Topson rose.

'We'll never get all this stuff into the truck,' he said. 'There's piles more than when we got here.'

'All the grub goes in,' said Sheepridge, 'and the extra water I got and if there's anything left it'll be that bloody brothel chair of his.' Topson forced open the tin of bacon with a small Italian bayonet.

'He won't like that,' he murmured.

'Then he'll sodding lump it,' said Sheepridge. 'Shut it off, and let me get on with me scriving.'

Crompton emerged from his wet sandstorm and found it cold. But, oh yes, this was the real nightmare. England. He shivered. A cold November wind rattled the windows.

'Well, mother,' he said calmly. 'I'm not exactly the first member of the family to be cashiered, I mean, darling, I do know the family history, God help me!'

'Not for theft, never before for theft!' said Lady Baysley harshly.

'Borrowing, darling, borrowing,' he said, lighting a cigarette. Under the carefully-regulated silver coiffure, her forehead was wrinkled, the eyes dark-circled. Gin, mostly, of course.

'I fancy kedgeree,' he said, moving to the sideboard. 'Mother?'

'It would choke me,' she said. No appetite. Gin, mostly.

'No wonder Catherine left you,' said his mother.

'No connection,' he murmured, filling his plate. 'No connection at all. Purely personal, as you know.'

Gilt-framed, in his Skinner's Horse uniform, Grandfather looked down ravenously at the sideboard. The rain beat against the window and Crompton shivered again.

Topson removed his earphones.

'Seven-thirty,' he said. 'Wireless silence until seven-thirty.'

'That's it, then,' said Sheepridge. He put down his writing-pad with an air of finality. Must have written fifteen pages in that careful hand of his. What did he put in those letters, Topson wondered.

'That's it, then,' said the driver again. 'When you open up again, that's it. Back to the Div. and then, Leeds, here I come!'

Where will he eventually get his letter off, Topson wondered. When will they collect the mail next? He saw a mirage containing a red pillar-box, perhaps, emerging in the middle of the waste-land.

'I think I'll shave,' he said. Sheepridge looked at him.

'Don't overdo it, Art, mate,' he said solicitously. 'We're not in bloody Tripoli yet. You'll be wearing boots, next news.'

'This time, I think we shall get there all right, eh?' said Topson.

'Tripoli? We'll get there,' said Sheepridge. 'Shan't be bloody back, neither. Goodbye Cairo and Alex, goodbye Canal Zone, goodbye Shaft's flaming cinemas, goodbye wogs!'

'Europe, then,' mused Topson. 'Greece, Italy?'

'Roll on Leeds!' shouted the driver. 'Can you 'ear me, mother? We've done buggering up and down the desert like a flaming fiddler's elbow!'

Topson glanced down at the sleeping figure.

'Well, *he* won't like that,' he remarked.

'Then he can sodding stay here, eh?' said Sheepridge, putting his letter carefully on top of his writing-case. 'He's never had no mail since we've been with him. Twelve months and not a letter. Got no home.' Topson sighed. 'And we don't even know his real name, not after twelve months. Funny, isn't it?'

'Bloody stupid if you ask me,' muttered the driver.

'We know he was cashiered in '38,' said Topson, 'and remember that brigadier in Abbassia stopping us and calling him Francis?'

'Francis bloody Drake, like as not,' said Sheepridge. 'A nob he is. You can tell. He can stay here if he likes. If he likes it so much.'

A smell of Nile water and some unidentifiable blossom came through the windows of the moored houseboat. Hospital. Hospital annexe. A houseboat on the Nile.

'Vera!' he said, *'don't tell me a ministering angel* thou, *of all people!'*

'*What are you doing here, Francis?*'

'*Jack*,' he said. '*Jack Crompton. Suffered a sea-change into something poor and strange. Concussion and liver trouble at the moment.*'

Fatter than when he last saw her. Came out in '36. With Catherine. Pals. She told him Catherine was commissioned in the WAAF. Often asked about him.

'*If you come across her in the wilderness of this world, darling*,' he said. *And gave her his name, number and Unit.*

'*Why should she want to contact* you *again? I wonder she doesn't start divorce proceedings, stupid girl*,' said Lady Baysley. His mother was standing behind the bed. She was in evening-dress.

'*Frankly darling*,' he murmured, '*it's none of your business. After all, you did die in '39.*' *Gin, mostly.*

The sky was pearl-coloured over the desert and the truck was packed. 'I give him ten minutes, said Sheepridge, 'and then we shove him in head first. Christ, he'll have a mouth like a camel's arse when he comes to.'

'I think he's moving a bit,' said Topson.

He was walking uneasily through strange surroundings. A crescent-shaped white beach enclosed shallow blue water, a walled Arab town was behind him, red-hatted and grinning Senegalese troops passed him on the dusty road, a chatter of Arabic and French filled his ears, as they clambered aboard their overloaded open trucks, plagued by Arab boys for sweets or cigarettes. He turned suddenly and encountered Catherine in tweeds. England closed around him.

'*You're forty-one, Francis*,' she said. '*Forty-one! If I'm ready to start again, why shouldn't you be! I've nothing to reproach myself with, God knows. The war's over, Francis, over! Father can get you a directorship and he's prepared to, even after all that's happened.*'

'*What has happened?*' he asked innocently. '*What has happened, Caterina mia?*'

'*If you could stop drinking it would make a start*,' she said. '*A new start. The war's over, over!*' . . . *She was gone.* . . . *On the flaking wall of the strange town a poster carried the portrait of a stern Churchill.* '*Justice doît être fait et il sera implacable*,' he was announcing.

'He's waking up,' said Topson.

'Christ, the sleeping beauty,' said Sheepridge, drawing his rifle from its sacking cover and eyeing it doubtfully. 'Some bugger give him a kiss, quick!'

Tall and lean and red eyed, Crompton rose unsteadily. He wore a sweat-stained blue Indian shirt and a pair of Afrika Korps trousers.

'Tea?' he queried.

'Flaming heck!' shouted Sheepridge. 'Everything's flaming packed, Sergeant mate, and we're off in five minutes. Tea!'

'Off,' said Crompton. He considered the word, 'Oh, *off*!' he said. 'Yes, the Big Push. Gentlemen in England now abed and all that. Yes.'

'We've even packed your bloody brothel chair,' said Sheepridge. 'Going to dump it but we thought we might flog it to the wogs somewheres.' Crompton stretched himself painfully.

'You will do nothing of the sort with that article of furniture which I requisitioned from the Governor of Benghazi,' he said. 'In the unhappy event of this war actually ending I may then return it to a legitimate Italian government. Meanwhile, it goes with me, Driver-Mechanic Sheepridge.' He looked around in the dim light. 'One thing that will not go with us,' he said, 'is Ludwig's helmet. Which you have been keeping the tea in. That must go back on top of his old rugged, German cross. Otherwise, when we come back this way in the near future, he may well ambush us.'

'We aren't coming back, this time, Sergeant mate,' snapped Sheepridge. 'Not this bloody time.' Crompton looked at him coldly.

'Don't be ridiculous, Percy,' he said. 'Of course, we'll be back. It is our destiny to go back and forth until the desert blossoms like a rose!' He looked at Topson. 'Jesu Cristo, Arthur!' he cried. 'You've shaved! This is a bad omen. Don't tell me *you* think this is the last time?' Topson nodded sheepishly. Crompton sat down heavily on the step of the truck. 'Et tu, Art!' he murmured. 'The road to Aldershot!'

'Some of us has homes to go to,' muttered Sheepridge. Crompton smiled.

'One day, you'll miss the desert,' he said softly.

'Miss the desert!' shouted the driver, kicking a rear tyre speculatively. 'Hear that, Art? Miss the sodding desert! Flaming roll on!' He picked up the helmet and poured the tea into a grey sock. 'Miss the desert!'

'Miss the desert,' repeated Crompton. 'One day, when the world is at peace and Johnny has gone to sleep in his own blasted room again or something and the kids are crying and all those lovely little peace-time problems are creeping around you and people are asking which road they ought to take, you'll miss the desert. Only one road here, eh. Runs East to West. Or West to East.'

'Give him a flaming camel, someone,' muttered Sheepridge.

'It's time,' said Topson.

'All right,' the driver shouted. 'Pick up your parrots and monkeys and fall in facing the boat!' Crompton picked up the helmet. They watched him as he walked slowly towards the grave.

'Mad,' said Sheepridge, 'flaming bonkers!' Topson said nothing.

'If we *are* going to bloody Sicily,' said Sheepridge, loading the last water container, 'why don't we go from *here*, why not go from Tunisia instead of buggering all the way back to Tripoli?'

'A prettier way round?' suggested Topson. The driver spat contemptuously.

'Roll on Leeds, anyways,' he remarked.

'Wonder what Johnny Crompton would be saying now,' Topson murmured. Sheepridge made no reply. 'Funny how they never *did* find his body,' Topson said.

'Found his bloody gear on the sodding beach, didn't they?' Sheepridge snapped. 'What more d'you want, found his gear on the beach.'

'He was a good swimmer,' said Topson, 'first-class. Sea's so calm here.'

'We've had all that before,' snapped Sheepridge. 'He's gone. Full of sodding wog brandy, he was, as usual. Give us a rest about Johnny Crompton, Art, for Christ's sake!'

Topson looked up at the roof of the truck. Under the bundled scrim-net, a slender gilt chair-leg remained uncovered.

'You never flogged his chair in the end, did you?' he remarked. Sheepridge turned away and waved towards the head of the line of vehicles.

'We're off,' he said shortly and climbed into the cab.

Slowly the convoy edged forward, passing a group of grinning Senegalese troops in their red hats, standing beside their over-loaded open vehicles. Slowly the truck moved into the town. From the flaking wall, Churchill on his poster gazed down on the dusty vehicle. 'Justice doît être fait et il sera implacable,' he announced.

RICHARD BEIOLEY

Plant Talk

A beautiful June day. The white puffs of cloud punctuating the
blue backdrop, gently shuffled by the whims of a capricious
summer breeze. A day for lounging around in back-yards. An
afternoon to be punctuated only by the chink of ice-cubes
settling comfortably in frosted glasses, the twang of tennis balls
bouncing off tightly-strung gut, and the overpowering scent of
English garden flowers.

Paul slammed the tailgate of the Volvo, closure on the second
attempt, and trudged unhappily along the crunchy gravel towards the house. She would be there, in the kitchen or perhaps
strutting from bedroom to bedroom, more than a hint of disapproval in her otherwise pretty face. She didn't need to say, 'I
never wanted to move here in the first place,' that much was
obvious and anyway they'd already been through all that a
thousand times.

He dumped the heavy suitcases by the imposing oak door,
paused, sifted through the silence. Nothing. Such a peaceful house,
such a tranquil setting. So what if she doesn't like it here? Big deal.
I've been doing what she wanted for years and now it's my turn.

The door was open, he struggled in with the cases, sensing her
presence almost immediately. He didn't look up, composing
himself mentally. No arguments, no ill-feeling. He was happy,
and what made him happy should make her happy too. That was
what marriage was all about, surely?

'Is that the lot then?'

She stood framed in the doorway of the dining-room, already wearing the face reserved for fighting.

'Yes, just about. I'll finish the last few odds and ends tomorrow. What I want right now is a long cool drink and a cigarette, then I think I'll do a bit of exploring—never know what you might find in these old houses.'

He paused, studying, hoping for evidence of interest, but found only cynicism.

'Well, all I want's a hot bath. A simple enough request in any *normal* house. Perhaps you could arrange some hot water?' God, he thought, some people can wear a frown like it was part of their make-up.

'No problem. I'll do it right away.'

'Good.' She stubbed her cigarette in the Wedgwood ashtray.

'And while you're about it, get the downstairs loo working. All I can say is things had better improve because I don't think I can stand this God-forsaken place too long otherwise. Have you *seen* the bathroom?'

She pauses to light another Rothmans. He had seen her do this countless times during their eight years together, but he still sees in this simple action a certain style, the way she always looks at something else while touching the lighter flame to the white cylinder bobbing up and down from the corner of her mouth. He always expects her to say, 'You know how to whistle, Steve, you just put your lips together and blow.'

'Paul, are you listening?'

He returns to reality.

'Of course. Look, don't worry, everything will be OK, just needs a little time, that's all.'

'Sure.'

Large gin-and-tonic in one hand, he stood before the panelled door leading to the cellar. He turned the handle and pushed, it

opened on to a dark staircase leading into Stygian gloom. He
looked above the door, just to make sure there wasn't 'Abandon
all hope, Ye who enter here' emblazoned gothically on the lintel,
smiled and reached for the light switch. The dusty cobwebbed
bulb gave barely adequate illumination. He descended the rickety
wooden staircase, half expecting to disappear in a cloud of rotten
timber at the next step. Surprisingly cool, a pleasant sensation.
Good place for keeping beer. That was one of the things he'd
promised himself, to brew good beer, lots of it, and this was the
perfect setting. Of course Helen wouldn't approve, but that's just
tough.

He scanned the cellar. Nothing of any great interest, almost a
film-set, so typically cellar-like were its contents: an old broken
chair, an empty crate, a splintered work bench leaning at a crazy
angle. He kicked the crate, recoiling from the mushroom cloud
of dust, turned to examine a pile of old newspapers, hoping for
an interesting antique headline, 'Lusitania Sinks' or somesuch.
In the shadows was a pot. He paused, bent and picked it up. A
plant pot and sprouting from the centre of the dried and crusty
humus was what appeared to be a dead plant. The stem withered,
it drooped slightly, brown crinkled leaves almost touching the
base. Odd, even though it gave no sign of vitality he sensed
something, some dormancy in its pathetic appearance, and
instead of putting it down again to be forgotten once more, he
turned and carried it back up the steps, walked absentmindedly
into the kitchen.

She turned from her noisy efforts with the sink plunger.

'Well, find anything?'

'No, nothing to speak of.'

'What's that then?' pointing with the dripping plunger.

'What, this? Just an old plant of some kind. Wants a bit of
tender loving care.'

She examined it suspiciously.

'Looks about as worn out as the rest of this place if you ask
me.'

(Well, I didn't did I, so shut your mouth.)

The parched soil soaked up what seemed like a huge volume of water. He stood the pot on an old plate, opened the kitchen door and placed it carefully on the cracked flagstones outside. On impulse he crouched down beside the misbegotten shoot, whispered conspiratorially, 'C'mon. Let's see what you can do. If only to spite ratface in there.'

The plant did not reply.

The following morning was a template for a summer's day. He dressed to the peaceful hum of bees inspecting the thick foliage outside the bedroom window. A gentle breeze rustled through season-proud silver birch, nothing else, no taxis, horns, pedestrian prattle. He felt the need for bacon and eggs.

'If you want a cup of tea, you'll have to go down to the village shop as the bloody milkman has obviously given this place a wide berth. Very sensible in my opinion.'

'Good morning, darling. Another beautiful day.'

Sunlight she wore like an ill-defined halo, her clothes moulded perfectly to the lithe body. What a pity the whole was governed by such an acutely dislikeable person. How typical of his questionable fortune to have fallen for such a woman.

'I feel like a stroll anyway. You get the breakfast going and I'll be back in fifteen minutes. OK?'

She switched on the radio.

Stepping outside the back door he nearly tripped over the plant pot, or was it the same one? Surely this erect firm stem, the skin fleshy and slightly waxy to the touch, was not his find of the previous day? He gently examined the uppermost leaves, unfurled now, glossy green flags, with radiating veins of pale yellow. He could almost feel the new vigour pulsating through their tiny capillaries.

At the sink, filling a small jug with cool water. The pot-earth dry again, needed replenishing.

'I thought you'd gone to the shop.' No reply.

'Paul, I'm talking to you.' She followed him out, watched him bend down, whispering. 'Is that the plant you found? Ugly looking thing, isn't it?'

He wheeled round, a curl of unreasonable anger in his taut smile.

'What the hell would you know about it?'

'All right, all right. Sorry I spoke. Didn't realise you were so sensitive, you'll be singing to it next.'

'I'm going for the milk.' He pointed to the pot. 'Leave that alone, understand?'

'Joanna and David said they might drive out at the week-end.'

'That'd be nice.' They parried over a less than cordial evening meal.

'Well, you don't have to be quite so enthusiastic about it, for Chrisake. After all, they're only our closest friends, the only ones, I might add, who've even halfway offered to come all the way out here to see us.'

'Just goes to show what the rest are worth then, doesn't it?'

He held the Niersteiner up to the fading rays of sun edging sheepishly through the leaded windows.

'A toast. To absent friends.'

'Sarcasm doesn't become you, and anyway, I thought you'd be pleased to talk to someone else besides that flaming rubber plant.'

The leaves had all opened. He fondled them gently, marvelling at the freshness and apparent youth. Did people suddenly develop green fingers? It was restful in the study, away from Helen.

Strange how the dark green surface of each leaf had a mottling of lighter yellowish patches. What was the word for it? Variegated? No. Something to do with chlorophyll distribution anyway, and attractive too. Rather like studying clouds, or the flames of an open fire, making pictures where none exist. Like that leaf there, the top one. What does that remind you of? A horse's head perhaps, over to the left. A letter P actually. How odd, because the shape next to it could so easily be a badly formed A. He blinked, looked away, giving the figures his mind had conjured a chance to disperse, then scrutinized the leaf again. They were still there, to the left of them a very passable U.

A little cold trickle of sweat ran down his spine, beneath the loose cotton shirt. To the right of the leaf was a final yellow patch. A bold downward stroke, a right angle at the base, less well defined. An L, a bloody L. He turned to yell for Helen, caught the sound, choked it back. Suppose she couldn't see it, or worse, pretended she couldn't?

The neat scotch went down easily. After five minutes he re-examined the leaf. PAUL. No argument.

He examined the next one down, a slight tremor in his hand disturbed the foliage. Immediately he deciphered a T, another A and an L, all unmistakable. The final letter was very vague. Possibly an R, no, a K. TALK.

'You want me to talk to you.' Not a question, merely a statement. 'Frankly, this has all come as a bit of a shock. You see, it's one thing me giving you a little verbal encouragement when you're down on your luck, but really it's quite another holding an intellectual conversation, which is potentially two-way, even if it does take a little longer than usual to hear your side of things.' He paused, searching for inspiration.

'The best thing we can do is get you absolutely fit first, give you the best of everything, food, sunlight etc. Perhaps you could give me a few hints there; after all, I'm a bit new to this game myself.'

A muffled cough outside the study door.

'That's her. Not a word. OK?'

The door opens.

'What are you up to? I thought I heard talking.'

'Who would I be talking to, goddammit?'

'Oh, I don't know,' she shrugs. 'That thing perhaps.'

'Don't be so bloody stupid, woman.'

Paul Donovan, writing his name at the top of a blank sheet of A4. Fantasizing on paper. Communication by plants: A treatise. He begins:

'It is said that long ago, in days now cobwebbed and forgotten, amidst sunsets like blood smeared on azure porcelain, that the prepubescent earth bore but a thick green mantle of vegetation, untroubled by the patter of prehistoric feet.

'Did this varied and wholly successful phylum really lie back in blissful ignorance, undisturbed by the neo-natal paroxysms of each emergent, blundering evolutionary step? Was there really no discussion, no intellectualizing, on a plane the level of which we have no conception, between these herbaceous first colonists? It is facile to point out that no such communicative ability exists merely because we have not experienced it. It begs the question; perhaps the plants have no desire to commune with a race which devotes considerable energy to destroying them, by burning them, eating them and chopping and poisoning in staggering proportions.

'Has a single, lone representative of this mighty and venerable order finally reached out the stem of friendship to mankind?'

A sleepless night. Towards dawn he drifts into a green limbo, tendrils of soft cellulose insinuating through chest-high herbaceous borders. A strange land of flowering plants, hedges and trees through which he floats, chattering inanely and deciphering cryptic messages on countless leaves.

He awoke with a start, sweat encased, the sun in his eyes, blinking at the reality of those two little words. Dressed hurriedly, no shave, and ran downstairs study-bound. The leaves proclaimed as loudly as before, though the letters seemed smudged now, nonetheless to him as clear as newsprint. A lower leaf caught his eye, a practised eye that quickly sorted the three pale shapes. SUN. He flung back the drapes joyously, let the sunlight pour its rejuvenating photons on the hungry chlorophyll.

'Take as much as you need,' he stroked the stem affectionately. A mental address. The Royal Society.

'Gentlemen, you see before you the greatest single step forward in botanical development since photosynthesis. I have here evidence of . . .' He must have evidence, drawings, notes, measurements. The day passes.

'Don't you want something to eat? Since when have you been so interested in plants? You haven't spoken to me in days, for God's sake.'

The observations, the studying, became obsessive. On day six he detected a change. It looked a little weak, a little dry perhaps. He increased, carefully monitoring, the water uptake, desperately hoping for another word, a clue to the subject's requirements. The stem bowed under the heavy foliage, he wanted to trim, to lighten the load, but didn't dare, too close to amputation. That night there was no sleep. Six-thirty found him standing numbly before the pot. A new message, on a leaf already beginning to crinkle at the edges. Three badly formed letters. DIE.

Fungicides, bio-nutrients, inorganic trace elements, and finally in a last-ditch attempt, re-potting in finest loam. The patient was sinking fast. In three days all but one leaf had curled and dropped, and with each fall, his heart fell also. On the morning of the fourth day of agony he knew it was all over. The smell of death lay heavy in the study. He touched the lonely leaf, saw the message there through tears of profound misery. Wept long and hard, blame and self-pity of an intensity he had not thought himself capable. At least there were no more tears to cry. He picked up the remains, strode through the kitchen, past a silent wife, and made for the top of the unkempt garden.

When the fire was going well, crackling loudly, he consigned the dry stem and leaves to the greedy flames. And then the last leaf. Without looking again at the spindly letters he dropped it and turned away. LOVE. The last word from a dying companion.

'Look, Paul, this is ridiculous. For God's sake, it was only a joke. I had no idea you'd carry it this far.'

He eyed her suspiciously.

'I mean, I thought you'd see the funny side of it, you know, plants talking through their leaves and all that. Obviously I over-estimated your sense of humour.'

A silence.

'You mean you did it?'

'Christ! You didn't think the plant did it?'

Fists rhythmically clench.

'That is the most profoundly ugly trick. How typical!'

'My God, you must be gullible!'

He turned to face her and she took a step back, unsure of his reaction.

'How did you do it?'

'Bleach, diluted a bit of course. Quite clever, I thought.'

'Quite clever. You selfish bitch. You were jealous of a sad old plant so you killed it.'

He stared up the garden.

Outside, shadows cast by the bright sun wandered across the lawn as the day went about its business. Towards the top, the heat haze shimmered through wisps of smoke from a small fire. Presently the fire died and the air was still again.

DOUGLAS DUNN

Do It Yourself

'Wait for it,' Bryan Harris told himself as he stood behind his front door. 'Wait for it.' Empty bottles chinked as the milkman put them into his wire crate. A dull, glassy thud followed as two full milk bottles were placed on Harris's doorstep. He cocked an ear towards the stairs.

'Bryan! I think that's the milkman!' his wife shouted from bed, surrounded by the Sundays which Harris had affectionately taken up to her ten minutes before.

'Yes, dear,' he said, making a face, 'I think it is.'

Ashamed of his inelegant dressing-gown and the Technicolored pyjamas which did not fit him, Harris swiped the bottles from the doorstep in the crouch of a man who does not want to be seen.

'Usual Sunday breakfast, darling?' he shouted up the stairs. He listened; he wondered if Georgina's silence was deliberate. 'I said, usual Sunday breakfast?'

'Do I have to write you a menu?' she shouted back.

Sunday breakfast meant two boiled eggs, instead of one; it meant butter on Georgina's toast instead of polyunsaturated marge; and it meant top-of-the-milk on her cereal instead of skimmed. It also meant the second instalment of their twice-weekly how's-your-father.

'Truly,' Harris said to the cat, 'it's Sunday morning. Next thing I know, she'll decide to have hard toilet paper six days a week, and soft on Sundays.'

Harris looked out at his back garden while the coffee filtered.
On Wednesday, his goldfish pond had dried up in mysterious
circumstances. He came home from work to find a hollow of grey,
drying concrete with, in the middle, a single fish the cat had left
for Mr Manners. Harris scratched his uncombed hair with fore-
boding. He had married into a clan of D.I.Y. experts; four of them
were coming for Sunday lunch. They'd have plenty to say about
his evaporated waterhole. The decorative heron that stood at its
edge seemed to be staring at the parched concrete hole with one
leg raised in livid frustration.

On his way upstairs with Georgina's tray the toe of his loose
slipper caught the inside of his drooping pyjama trouser-leg. He
slid downstairs on his belly and knees, trying to hold the tray
steady.

'Bryan!'

'Sorry, dear,' he whimpered, picking a slice of toast from the
wall.

Harris's in-laws and all their progeny were dissatisfied with
him. 'Put the light on, Bryan, would you? You do this with the
switch,' it was gestured, 'ha ha ha.' Harris was radically displeased
with them but their practical, dexterous piety was unassailable.
His father-in-law was the sort of man who could put in a new
window before breakfast, mow the lawn, go to church, repair the
vacuum cleaner while his Sunday lunch was being cooked, take a
nap, and then repair the roof.

Once inside his house, Harris's restless father-in-law and his
deceptively jovial in-law uncle subjected it to what looked like a
systematic survey conducted in a series of fidgets.

'Fitted carpets,' said the uncle, 'hide a multitude of sins.' For a
moment Harris feared that the carpets were coming up. 'I hope
you had a good look at the boards before you laid that.' Harris
assured them he had; in fact, the carpets had been laid by a fitter
from the shop where he bought them.

'Are you a member,' his father-in-law asked, picking up the
new *AA Members' Handbook*, 'of this?' Harris was a member of

both motoring organizations. He dreaded a breakdown. In his opinion, the number of wayside emergency telephones was distressingly inadequate. He had nightmares about having to open the natty metal toolbox, his motorist's repair kit—a Christmas present from Georgina—and discover what was inside that might be of use to whatever hearty, interfering benefactor stopped to ask if he needed any help. 'I'll take a look at your car.'

'It's in for its service,' Harris said.

'What?' his father-in-law said. He seemed sincerely upset that a son-in-law of his resorted to garages.

'In all my years of motoring,' said Arthur, disappointed in Harris as much as he was proud of himself, 'I've never, never allowed these garage mechanics to touch, to so much as look at, any of my cars.' Harris shrugged.

'Arthur,' said Uncle Ted, 'Bryan wouldn't know where to start.'

Uncle Ted could make anything, including turnip wine: he had a complexion to prove it. He smelled of aftershave suppressed by an aroma of industrial fluid used to clean grease from the hands. Bored, he switched on the TV set. As both he and Arthur suspected, its controls were crying out for adjustment.

'Too much green,' said Arthur, as earnest as an art critic, his eyes narrowing, and his face screwed up as if on a sour taste.

'Too much blue?' Uncle Ted suggested. More delicate movements of the switches followed.

'You're back to green, Ted.' Taking a suitable screwdriver from his jacket pocket, Harris's father-in-law removed the protective grille at the back of the set. In spite of all warnings to the contrary, the set remained on; a programme for Pakistani viewers was in progress. Relishing the prospect of his father-in-law done to a crisp in front of the jabbering objects of his casual bigotry, Harris sat back with a newspaper. Both Uncle Ted and Arthur charred into one mutual, human, sizzling flake was too much to hope for: but he did not want that, because he knew it would leave him the man of the family.

'Spot on, Ted!' They rubbed their hands and screwed the grille back into place.

'Nig-nogs! Look, Arthur, nig-nogs!' Arthur switched it off; he looked for something else to fix.

'Oh, God, no, not now, please, please,' Harris lamented inwardly, like bad mental wind. Arthur, sniffing out things to occupy him, had reached the French doors that opened into the garden. It was a mess compared to his own; Harris's inexpert but conscientious gardening almost made Arthur weep. Uncle Ted wet his lips, winked, and wet his lips again.

'Drink, Ted?'

'I wouldn't say no, Bryan.'

Harris had observed Uncle Ted in his natural habitat. Among perfect workmanship lavished on bad taste, Uncle Ted would sit in his armchair within ordering distance of the black leatherette bar with gold studs which he had built into a corner of his living-room. At the side was a hand-made bookcase containing volumes of adventure stories in what Ted believed were fine bindings and bought by mail order.

'Arthur? What about you?'

'What's wrong with this door?' Arthur asked, indignant, and puzzled; he was not used to door-handles that did not work without coaxing.

'You lift it a bit, and then push,' Harris said. Lifting more than was necessary and pushing harder than he needed to, Arthur barged his way into the garden. Uncle Ted downed his Scotch and scuttled after his brother.

'What's Daddy doing?' his mother-in-law asked in the over-staffed kitchen.

'Daddy's doing his nut,' said Harris, clearing the steamed windows to reveal two pond inspectors. He was always sure of sympathy from his mother-in-law and his in-law aunt. Georgina said, 'I told you, you should have asked Daddy to help you instead of trying to do it yourself. And look what happened.'

'Act of God,' said Harris. Georgina had offered to dig the pond herself when Harris tried to abort the operation half-way through. It had goaded him on, that imagined moment of his neighbours watching from their upstairs windows as his wife dug a large hole in the garden and mixed the cement to fill it.

'Arthur!' his mother-in-law shouted from the window. 'Dinner!' It was like tapping a spoon on a plate before a hungry cat. It was like a dinner gong struck in a seaside boarding-house. Uncle Ted dropped the hose he had been unwinding, preparing it for an experiment to find out where the leak was. 'Arthur!' said Harris's mother-in-law, and Arthur wiped his feet, then washed his hands obediently at the sink. Uncle Ted stood behind him like a small queue.

'Now go through it again.' Harris thought he might have a chance to eat something, but he was obliged to withhold his fork as, once more, he went through each stage of his pond-building process. 'Now,' said Uncle Ted, 'what did you forget to do?' He winked at Arthur.

'Leave Bryan alone,' said his in-law aunt. Arthur passed over the bit that Bryan was supposed to have missed out. Harris suspected that Arthur didn't know a pond from a hole in the ground.

'Do you have a pick?' Uncle Ted asked.

'A pick? No, of course I don't have a pick.'

'It'll have to be broken up,' Arthur said with his mouth full, 'dug up, chipped out, and removed.'

'You'll need a wheelbarrow,' said Ted, savouring his turnip wine.

'I've got a barrrow,' said Harris. 'At least, I've got a barrow.'

'That's a diddy-barrow. You'll need a man's barrow.'

'And planks,' said his father-in-law.

'Planks?'

'Planks,' said Uncle Ted, 'to run the barrow on, or you'll rut your lawn.'

'I wouldn't call that a lawn, Ted. Of course, you'd save time with a pneumatic drill,' said his father-in-law. Harris shuddered pneumatically at the very thought. It was bad, imagining his neighbours watch him as he undid two week's labour with a pick; but it was worse, much worse, picturing them with their up-turned noses and whispered remarks behind their bedroom curtains as he jumped up and down at the mercy of a pneumatic drill. Arthur washed down his advice with a gulp of Ted's Hock-type turnip wine.

After dinner, Uncle Ted ran the hose on the pond.

'A very slow seepage,' Arthur said, 'very slow.' To Harris it looked as if it wasn't leaking at all.

'It must have been one of those things,' he said. 'It isn't leaking.'

'The birds,' said Uncle Ted, with a punishing command of the facts, 'didn't drink it. Oh, it's leaking all right.'

'There's no swirl on the water,' said Harris desperately.

'Not at the moment,' said Arthur, with the deep, melancholy voice of a born handyman passing judgement on a mistake, 'but there will be.'

Leaving Harris to roll up the hose, Arthur and Uncle Ted began to repair the lock and handle on the French windows. These were one of the reasons why the Harrises had bought the house.

'Oh, look, Bryan, French windows!'

'I've always known it,' Harris said to himself as he watched Arthur and Uncle Ted at work, 'these blasted doors have been a downer on me ever since I bought the place.'

It took a long time before his father-in-law and his in-law uncle were ready to re-fit the several component parts of the locking mechanism and the door-handle.

'Tea's up!' shouted his mother-in-law. Both workers straight-ened their backs and seemed to put their jackets on in one move-ment while also taking the first unhesitating step towards tea.

'Tea,' said Arthur.

'Tea,' said Uncle Ted.

'What about the doors?' Harris asked, fearing the worst.

'You'll have that back together in no time,' said Uncle Ted.

'You do it,' said his father-in-law.

'Do it yourself,' said Arthur, not unkindly, but with a hint that he felt he had done enough for one day. After the goodbye ritual at the door, Georgina said, 'I've been asking you about these doors for months.'

'Have you seen them? Have you seen the state they've left them in? Well, have you?'

'You watched them take that lock apart, so surely you know how to put it together again, Bryan.'

'It looks like the insides of a Swiss watch!'

'I know, dear,' she said, 'they're trying, and the doors weren't all that bad, but I don't know how to fix a lock.' Harris nodded with gratitude for Georgina's sympathy. He sat down for a rest on the assumption that if he had one now he wouldn't need one later on.

'Daddy thought we'd made a very good job of the bathroom,' she said.

'Really?'

'And he asked what the marks were on the stair carpet.' Harris frowned.

'I rubbed, and rubbed,' he said. 'I hoped they'd dry out. Have we any stain remover?' he asked, getting to his feet.

'Not now, darling. I told him it was me. I didn't want him getting on at you.'

'You'd think it was his house.'

'I know, dear.'

Harris worked at the French doors until it got dark. He took up one screwdriver, put it down, took up another, and still the infernal object would not fit together, or, when it did, it would not match the space in the door it had been taken from.

'People shouldn't leave jobs unfinished,' he shouted to Georgina who was watching television at the other end of the room. 'If they have the cheek to chop up other people's houses, then they might have the decency to finish what they start.'

Lamps were rearranged to illuminate his work. The cat stole across the lit green of the lawn, followed by another. Georgina said she was going to bed.

'There were two of them, you know. And there's only one of me.'

'Is it tricky?'

'Good God, woman, it's midnight, and you ask, Is it tricky?'

'There's no need to shout.'

At two in the morning, Harris stood back and appraised his work. The paintwork was chipped and scored around the handle and the metal covering which surrounded the hole into which the tongue of the lock fitted. It looked unsightly. At least, you no longer had to lift and push. It worked perfectly. Time and again he opened the door, closed the door. The cat ran in; he patted it and it wanted out again: he opened the door and let it out. One gentle movement of the wrist was all it took. There was a click, soft, precise and deeply satisfying. He turned the key. He reached up and slid the top bolt; he bent down and slid the lower bolt.

'A pick,' he mused, 'or a pneumatic drill?' He drew the curtains. 'A pick shouldn't be difficult to get.'

CARYL BRAHMS

A Bouquet in the Ballet

A fine summer's day in the Marylebone Road, London W1. That is to say it was scarcely raining at all. A small moistish crowd had collected in the misty drizzle and stood gawping at the broad steps that dignified the would-be Palladian frontage of the Town Hall. What was happening on them, however, was of a romantic rather than classical nature, since Nadia Nijni-Novgarodova, Ballerina Assoluta to the Stroganov Ballet, was being handed down them, *sur les pointes*, by a short and definitely furious Bridegroom. The Bride was wearing full holy Russian bridal regalia, starting with the elaborate embroidered and jewelled head-dress (*Oiseau de Feu*) but ending abruptly in a tarlatan tu-tu. Behind the happy couple a quartet of Bridesmaids, resigned rather than radiant, showered them with paper rose petals as gracefully as their imbalance would permit. The on-lookers applauded apathetically, a little damply.

The Bride hurled rather than tossed last night's bouquet into their moist midst. The bouquet sailed on to hit the solitary police-man who had sauntered over from across the road to find out what was happening prior to ordering whatever it might be to move on. The crowd applauded the policeman too. Bored, the Bride-groom yawned. He had married the Bride before—in Sante Fé, Seattle, Salt Lake City, Munich, Marseilles, Manchester, Bridling-ton, Billingham and . . .

But at this point the spicing of rain, for this was an English

summer, turned into a right tropical downpour. Bride and Groom
abandoned their newly wedded bliss and dashed back up the steps
to shelter under the Palladian-type portico. So did the Bridesmaids—*sauve qui peut*. Meanly the camera went on clicking. So did
as many of the crowd as could insert themselves. So did the
policeman. And so did a broadly shouldered, broadly stomached,
bald and vigorously mopping man, hitherto beaming in the drizzle
at the happy pair.

'Stop shoving, Stroganov,' snapped the Matron of Honour,
Arenskaya, ballet mistress to the Stroganov company, whose
costume for this fantastic espousal seemed to have been borrowed
largely from Schéhérazade. 'Can you not see there is no room for
you?' She tried to push the impresario down the steps. 'Full up
on top,' essayed the jovial policeman. No one laughed at his joke.
No one ever did. Downright discouraging. The Bride did her
best to tug Stroganov back. His arms became a human windmill.
Balance regained, he rounded on his Assoluta.

'Me,' he protested, 'who have give you away in Leeds, where
the snow come down, in Woolomaloo, where the roof come
down, and in San Francisco where the world come down . . .'

'Olright! Olright! Olright!' The livid Bridegroom sought to
stem the flood. 'And,' he remembered, 'kindly to note, next time
I marry her you up me the salary'. He sneezed.

'Enough,' shouted the enraged Stroganov, '*ça suffit!* Already I
have paid the wedding you do not have, the reception you do
not have, the honeymoon you do not have . . .'

'Ah! Ça, non!' put in the Bride. She sniffed. The Bridegroom
disregarded the slight. Also the impresario, who was still in full
spate, '. . . And the nervous breakdown . . .'

'This I do have,' the reluctant Bridegroom smiled for the first
time that afternoon.

'So now we put on our galoshes and do the damquick get-away
or we are late for the matinée and the cut-the-wedding-cake for
the Press between shows.'

'The same cake,' the poorest girl in the Ballet, British of course, pointed out to the world in general.

At this point, the sun sailed out. The Bride blew a kiss to the shivering onlookers. The Bridegroom bowed. The policeman winked. Stroganov beamed.

Almost it might have been a Russian Wedding.

The florists around the corner from the Colodeum Theatre was named after its proprietors, the Two Ballerinas—not speaking— a privation to both, communicating their thoughts on the subject of each other's shortcomings, bilingually, in spidery writing on the back of odd scraps of wrapping paper and that after they had found their pens, was not at all the same thing.

This morning both Ballerinas were particularly busy. The Stroganov company's Assoluta, la Nijini-Novgarodova, had descended on them early to secure the best blooms for the best price for the best bouquet she would give herself, to receive on stage with wide-eyed surprise that night. 'I dance the new Nevajno—"*Caviare to the Heneral*" *très moderne!*' she told the Two Ballerinas.

'Aie!' they exlained as one Ballerina. They glared at each other.

'And remember,' Assoluta-Eyes-On-Stalks looked keenly at some wilting tulips, 'nothing but the best—and biggest—*and* cheapest, you get me!' They got her. They shrugged resigned shoulders. Almost they had become as sisters in what was plainly going to become the battle of the blooms. Money, it seemed, was no object when you were an Assoluta—your money, that was.

Fortunately their next customer was not an Assoluta—that would have been bankruptcy. She was in fact the poorest girl in the Ballet. And could the Rag Tag and Bobtail in the Stroganov company be poor! And though she took care of the pennies somehow she never seemed to have the pounds to leave to take care of themselves. What kind of a bouquet could she hope to buy herself for . . . conscientiously she counted . . . 40p? A big financial problem this. After a spirited haggle she settled for five

gladioli, nothing like as good as new, indeed definitely despon-
dent: and a straggle of what might be termed mountain greenery,
which might get by, at least from the gallery. The same thing went
for the ladder in her only pair of silk tights.

Alfie, the stage door-keeper at the Colodeum Theatre, where the
Ballet Stroganov was appearing ('It should have been the Covent
Garden,' Vladimir Stroganov informed the meagre gallery queue
hotly) allowed it to be known that it was his birthday—'Eighty-
nine and I'll never live to be ninety,' he wheezed. A corny
performance, but always good enough for a whip-round when a
new company came in. Yet none of the bouquets that filled his
torrid little den were for him—most of them were fated to be
eked out for a week.

Right now the avaricious Alfie was on his customary rounds
making sure that no saucer-eyed, warm-hearted little coryphée
failed to fork out in the whip-round, for it was well-known at the
Scroungers Club that the Ballet Stroganov was a soft touch.
'Ninety years young, they do say,' chunnered the stage door-
keeper, 'but I'll never live to see ninety-one,' he croaked, coughing
his most bronchial cough for good measure. His was a practised
performance.

Anatoly, the Town Hall Bridegroom and Premier Danseur to
the Ballet Stroganov, having flicked the dust from the laurel
wreath he always travelled with, and kicked his rival Oleg's laurel
wreath into the shades of night—for it always was murky night
in Alfie's office—beckoned the poorest girl in the Ballet to join
him. 'Kindly to note our coast is now clear, so come quick and
do the select.'

Theirs was a fast friendship of a non-emotional and cosy kind
that demanded nothing of either ally and so suited both temper-
aments. The poorest girl in the ballet kicked her chum's rival's
laurel wreath to show solidarity.

Her name was Ivy but she was not the clinging kind. She was

known to her enemies—and what would the ballet be without them?—as Poison Ivy. But this did the poor girl less than justice, for Ivy was abrasive rather than secretive. Poverty breeds fighters. She ran a practised eye over the bouquets, mentally pricing the blooms. 'This one,' she said, pointing inevitably to la Nijni-Novgarodova's flowers. The choice appeared to delight the much-married Bridegroom.

That sound of coughing and shuffling from the other end of the corridor could only herald the approach of Alfie. Mercifully he was intercepted by the owner of the much-kicked laurel wreath, doubtless with instructions to dust it off. 'Kindly to note we must do the damquick bunk,' urged Anatoly.

Quick as a Harlequin in a hurry he ripped off la Nijni-Novgarodova's card of good wishes to herself. Quick as a vanishing lizard's tail Ivy went to work on the card she had attached to her own impoverished floral tribute. Alfie's slow shuffle and his hacking cough could be heard coming nearer—no Harlequin he. Quick as the flick of an adder's forked tongue the transfer was completed.

'Kindly to note we must piss off,' urged the idiomatic Anatoly.

Together they got the hell out.

Still summer, but the venue has changed. A small group of citizens and one solitary well-wrapped-up tourist from Salt Lake City with nothing better to do and no inclination to do it were braving the bitter easterly wind that was whistling round the Brum Town Hall. A wedding, it seemed, was going on all down the broad stone steps. A Ballerina in full Russian bridal regalia cut short by a tu-tu was descending *sur les pointes*, handed down by a furious and unco-operative Bridegroom. 'Kindly to note this is the last time I marry myself to this woman, Stroganov. The last time I catch the pneumony in your bitter English Summer.' He sneezed. 'The last time I make of myself the damnfool Petrouska before your British Burgomeisterschloss!' *'Bien sûr, mon* ami,' said the placating impresario, to his vanishing premier danseur's coat-tails.

'I also!' shrilled the tottering Bride, blue with cold and robbed of her supposed spouse's support. She sneezed. She shied her bouquet at Stroganov, missed, and a gust of wind caught it and deposited it out of reach on a bronze statue of Austen Chamberlain, unexpectedly hoist on his own bronze. It was a truth universally accepted that his bronze eye-glass was exceptionally realistic.

'Aie! And they cost a package!' mourned the earth-bound Stroganov, gazing at the out-of-reach flowers aloft.

'And, said the poorest girl in the Ballet, fiendishly, to the nearest reporter's notebook, 'she cannot now present them to herself tonight and must buy another bouquet with choice flowers.' She gloated.

All that week changing the labels on presentation bouquets had become more than usually fraught. A Senior Citizen, an enthusiastic researcher into the subject of UFO's, a woolly-minded lady at the best, with the physical contours of a large black sitting hen, whose named appeared to be 'Stage Door Lady, Darling' was the chief danger. Stage Door Lady Darling seemed to be glued to her chair, waddling forth only at the call of nature and though her face was buried in the much-scored-through proofs for the *UFO Sentinel* over which she clucked endlessly, but our illicit callers never knew when she would look up to tend her perpetual cold in the nose.

'Kindly to note this Stage Door Lady Darling has the eye evil in the backside of her head.' The reluctant Bridegroom gave his rival's wreath a relieving kick.

'The flowers are not for you to kick,' said Stage Door Lady Darling. She sneezed. She wiped the drip off on the back of her hand. She had outer space on her mind.

'Oh well,' said the poorest girl in the Ballet, resigned to a week of straggling marigolds. She, too, kicked the unfortunate Oleg's laurel wreath.

Without raising her head, Stage Door Lady Darling wagged a remonstrating pen. It spluttered. 'I would report you and have you fined if I could pronounce your long Russian names.' She sniffed.

'Ivy Smith,' said Ivy Smith.

'Impertinence will nowhere get you,' warned a just-arrived Stroganov. He collected his mail and took it up to his office.

'Bill ... bill ... bill ... which I do not pay,' he promised himself. He brightened.

There was a knock at the door. 'Go away!' Stroganov called. Arenskaya came in.

'Vladimir, I have come to demand the rise.'

'But I give you the rise only five years ago,' he protested.

'But my darlink the inflation and the faithful service.'

'But the cost of touring. And the poor houses.'

'You owe it to my Art.'

'Maybe. But my darlink I have receive this morning all these bills.' He picked them up and shook them at her.

'*Eh bien!*' said the experienced Arenskaya, instantly resigned.

Silence descended on the long-time pair of allies—that is, when they were not being long-time adversaries. It was broken by a shriek of delight from Arenskaya. 'Eureka!' she crowed.

'Nu?'

'Next week we make the big economy. What you pay the 'appy pair to marry again in Veston-super-mare?'

'Plenty,' sighed Stroganov.

'So what, Vladimir? So you marry me!'

Stroganov's ruddy cheeks paled. He mopped his sweating brow.

'Me, I am faithful to my long-dead wife,' he announced.

'What long-dead wife?' asked Arenskaya, puzzled.

A virtuous smirk lit Stroganov's rounded countenance. 'The one I always meant to marry.

'Eh bien, mon ami, you save you the generous fee you give the 'appy couple, and you give to 'appy me! It is the solution clever, non?'

'No,' said Stroganov explosively.

'Me, I 'ave my Ballet Shoes from my Giselle, still.'

'Twenty years ago,' said Stroganov to the ceiling. '*Tiens!* They last well, those slippers, who made them?'

But Arenskaya's whole being was alight with the glow of a past glory. Clearly next week's Town Hall steps were to be her recaptured moment of *réclame*.

'Me, I mount *sur les pointes*, and you, you support me down the steps, and the afternoon is saved in Sunderland.'

'Come, my old, let us rehearse ourselves.'

A raw day in Sunderland. The sun shone, but fitfully. The clouds from time to time extinguished it.

The Ballet was rehearsing under the strict supervision of la Arenskaya.

'Stop! Stop! Stop!' she shrilled. 'And that means you, too!' she switched glares to the pianist, who oblivious to Arenskaya's red light, was carrying on thumping.

At the stage-door a tourist from Salt Lake City—where have we seen that plaid before?—was addressing the local Stage Door Keeper, Darling, without any noticeable effect. True she had looked up from *The Vegetarian Times* ('What to do with Rotten Cabbage') but only to sneeze.

'Mr Anatoly Karapek? I have some business to discuss with him. It will not detain him long,' the Tourist from Salt Lake City pleaded.

'Atishoo!' said the local Stage Door Keeper Darling accusingly.

'Atishoo!' said the Tourist from Salt Lake City. Evidently they were in complete cahoots on the vexing subject of summer colds.

The crowd of idlers who had assembled to watch the goings-on

on the steps of the Town Hall did not include the Tourist from
Salt Lake City—odd! But there was plenty going on at the
moment.

An elderly lady, dressed mainly in pearls, with rouged cheeks
and heavily mascaraed eyelashes was batting them at the fortunately phlegmatic Fuzz planted in her near vicinity. Beside her the
bald-domed, well-rounded stomached, excitable old gent was
comparing his wrist-watch with the clock on the War Memorial
every other minute. It told its owner the hour in most of the cities
of the world from Yokohama to York, but not the time in
Sunderland.

'They are late, our 'appy pair,' he informed Arenskaya.

'This I know,' said the old lady with the poker down her spine.
She rattled her pearls. A string broke. Pandemonium took place
as one and all tried to restore them to the little old lady with the
ballet shoes with which she was tapping one foot, calling out the
while, 'Up there, Vladimir, down there, Vladimir,' to the purple-
faced impresario who found it difficult to bend these days, even
on the flat.

And still no Bride—no Bridegroom. Up in the sky the sun
came out.

' 'Appy the Bride the sun shines on,' said Oleg, 'and Groom,'
he added. The sun winced and hid an embarrassed face behind a
baby cloud.

'And still they do not come,' said Stroganov for perhaps the
seventh time.

An urchin who had been trying to pierce the small knot of
onlookers now arrived at the bald-dome's elbow. 'For you, Guv,'
he piped, waving a purple envelope redolent of Mitsouko at the
impresario. Stroganov's bones misgave him. He tore open the
envelope. He fumbled in a pocket for his eyeglass. Read . . . Read
. . . Read . . . Re-read . . . Re-read . . . Re-read. Of what avail?
The ungrateful words were still there. The purple letter fluttered
from his hand and down to the steps. 'Gone,' he told Arenskaya.

'The 'appy couple?'

'Gone,' he repeated.

It had started to rain.

'*Laisse voir*,' said Arenskaya. Stroganov stooped—an achievement in itself.

Read ... Read ... Read ... and so on. Then she let out a shriek of laughter. 'The Ballet Lake Salt City! Fools!' she cackled. 'Do they not know they are all much married there?'

'They have left us. Gone!' mourned Stroganov.

'Gone,' agreed Arenskaya, 'to a land where they know not a *pas-de-bourré* from a *pas-de-basque*.'

'They'll be back,' said the consoling Fuzz. He took the letter and perused it. He got the message. No need to read a second time.

'We know that in this City of the Lake they wed themselves frequently, but it is not like your freezing British summer. There the sun shines. And they up us the salary.'

'They'll be back,' repeated the experienced Fuzz.

'*Alors*! Now you hand me down the steps,' said the impatient Arenskaya.

Not without effort the old ones took over. Arenskaya levitated to her creaky toes. Stroganov staggered slightly but handed her down and all without a catastrophe.

Kindly to note that the greater part of this story is true. Only in the Ballet could such things be. But who will believe me anyway?

STAN GEBLER DAVIES

Apotheosis of McFee

'Last I saw of him—in real life, that is,' McFee said, 'he was standing on the pavement outside the Closerie de Lilas making a meal out of the contents of his nose. Wearing one of his white suits as I recall. That would be April of 1939, just before the Sûreté fingered me collar. Caught me living off of a widder woman, called it blackmail, do you know. I was inside for the duration. Stroke of luck, if you come to think of it. Poor buggers on the outside getting their arses shot off, and myself snug inside and safe from the troubles of the world.'

'You are more like a character out of Beckett,' I said, 'than out of Joyce.'

He plucked from a plateful of sandwiches a triangular sliver of bread and smoked salmon. It halted a brief instant between plate and mouth, held between black fingernails.

'Funny thing about the blind,' he said. 'Have you noticed? Can't see what the other chap is up to, they think no one can see what *they're* up to. Hence the nose-picking. Jiyce was the divil for it. There is mention of it in *Ulysses*, do you know.'

This is true. Professor Ellmann has commented on it at length.

The smoked salmon passed over twin stumps of teeth. A waiter appeared behind McFee. 'Would sir require a finger bowl?'

'Sir would not,' said McFee, a sneer flitting over his face. 'Sir prefers to wipe his fingers on his shirt.' This he did. It had been his idea to have tea at the Ritz. 'I am not a character out of a book,' he said. 'I am myself.'

'You are,' I agreed, 'uniquely yourself.'

This remark appeared to please him. 'I am ready for a whisky now, I think,' he said. 'A stiff whisky.'

'The bar is closed,' the waiter said.

'In that case,' McFee said, 'allow me to invite you to my club.'

It was not far. The other side of Piccadilly Circus, in a basement near the French pub. We taxied. McFee's feet were no longer up to walking.

'Could you not shut that window?' McFee said in the cab after I had opened it. It was the tail end of November. 'No,' I said. There was a pong proceeding from his person that was more than faintly reminiscent of certain neglected cesspits I have come across in remote rural areas of the west of Ireland. 'I am an old man,' McFee said. 'You will have me in my grave.'

'Shut up,' I said.

Through a thick fug of cigarette smoke, unlaundered clothes and unwashed bodies were perceptible the hazy outlines of afternoon drinkers.

'Who the fuck are you?' said the barman, a short, fat, catamite with an ugly Ulster accent. 'He is with me,' McFee said.

'Who asked yew?' the catamite said. 'Have yiz money?'

I put five pounds on the bar and ordered whiskies.

'Large,' McFee said.

'Sit down, McFee,' I said, 'and get to the point. This is the last drink you are getting until you deliver the goods. Poindexter is losing patience.'

Poindexter, my publisher, had commissioned me to extract from McFee certain papers said to concern the late James Joyce and, if possible, utilise them in the composition of a new biography of the Irish master.

McFee withdrew slowly from under his coat a sheaf of rolled-up papers that were grimy and dog-eared. I held out my hand.

'I have no money left,' McFee whined. 'It is all spent.'

'That is too bad,' I said, hand still outstretched.

'I have not the rent. I will be on the pavement.'

'You were given fifty pounds last week.'

'It was stolen,' McFee said, his black rheumy eyes on me, 'be hoors.' At this he proffered the papers and I snatched them. I had been at pains to conceal my excitement but no longer did so.

'It's the real stuff,' McFee said.

Plainly, it was. The tortuous handwriting, reminiscent, as Joyce himself had remarked, of 'Napoleon Bonaparte the morning after Waterloo' was, after long hours spent poring over manuscripts in the BM Library, as familiar to me as the blackmailer's to his victim.

I could not bear to read, for the first time, this part of the work of the greatest writer of the century in the company of a wretch like McFee.

'I will take it home with me,' I said, quitting the vandalised bar stool. 'I will be in touch with you tomorrow.'

'You aren't leaving me,' McFee wailed, 'with no money?' Tears began to well at the corners of his blood-shot eyes. His voice quavered. 'An old man like me. They will put me on the pavement. I will not last the night.'

'Oh shut up,' I said. I tossed him ten pounds. The snivelling ceased.

'Tanks,' McFee said. 'Have a good read.'

By two in the morning I had come to the conclusion that I had in my possession a portion of the autobiography of James Joyce, looted, McFee claimed, from the Paris apartment of a dead German officer at the end of the war. This claim was indeed sustained by the fact that there were marginal comments scribbled in an elegant hand, in German, on the pages. The dead Kraut had evidently been a man of culture.

McFee had, cunningly, selected sheets from two quite diverse parts of the narrative. One dealt with *Finnegan's Wake* and the reception it got as Joyce released it piecemeal.

'I said it would take the professors a thousand years to unravel *Ulysses*,' was one of the less incendiary remarks, 'but they would not in a million years admit that *FW* was all a cod because if they did they would be out of a job.'

The next extract concerned Nora, Joyce's wife, and was scabrous in the extreme. Certain degraded images I could not cleanse from my mind after I had read it. I drank a good deal of brandy and fell into a fitful sleep . . .

The apparitions appeared to me in that hour which precedes waking, the hour of nightmares.

Joyce himself was as immediately recognisable to me as his handwriting had been. Immaculate in a white linen suit, he wore a black patch over the left eye and carried in his right hand an ash-plant walking stick. His wife, by his side, was the blowsy remains of a faded beauty, a cloche hat stuck on her dark red curls and the rest of her enveloped in an ill-fitting, sack-like garment that did, however, with its stench of money proclaim the couturier's art.

We were in the Champs Elysées.

'Good day,' I said.

Joyce halted his perambulation and turned the one ruined but still functioning eye upon me. 'Are you aware,' he said, 'that you address the author of *Ulysses*?'

'I am aware,' I said, 'that I have that honour.'

'Mind you watch your peas and queues,' Mrs Joyce said, in a thick Galway brogue.

'You will forgive my wife,' Joyce said. 'She is an ignorant woman, rescued by myself from the streets of Dublin. It is a fact that she has not got past page twenty-seven of my masterpiece, including the cover.'

'Come home now, Jim,' she said, pulling at his sleeve, 'and keep out of trouble.'

He raised his hat to me. 'You see how it is? I am a man of some modest genius but I am at the mercy of this peasant from Galway.'

'Come along, Jim.'

'Yes, Nora, my love.'

Off they went, into the crowd, she turning baleful eyes over her shoulder to me as she steered him away. 'Give up that book,' she hissed. 'Give it up!'

'What book?' I said.

'I'll give you what book,' she said, and swung her handbag at me. It struck me just above the elbow and I promptly woke up from the pain. A nasty bruise rose where the handbag had landed and persisted for some days.

McFee had been for twenty years installed in a fifth-floor garret in Campden Grove. The landlady would no longer venture beyond the third floor. 'You would need a gas mask,' she said.

I had drenched myself in the most powerful Cologne waters I could find. The protection this afforded me against the stench of McFee's den was, however, quite insufficient.

'By God,' I said. 'Could you not get the sanitation department to hose the place down?'

'They wouldn't come,' McFee said, 'and I wouldn't blame them. Did you bring the whisky?'

I handed him the bottle of cheap Scottish whisky he had demanded. He unscrewed the top and put the bottle to his mouth. 'It's me birthda tomorra,' he said.

'I understood,' I said, 'that your birthday was the second of February, 1882, the same as Joyce's. By the way, do you keep cats here?'

'There was a cat here wance,' McFee said, stroking his stubbled chin with nicotine-stained fingers, 'an owl black tom. Haven't seen the bugger for six months now.'

'It could be,' I said, 'that the animal expired and that you have failed to detect the corpse among the furniture.'

'Could be,' McFee said. 'I wouldn't put it past it. That business about the birthda's'—he paused a moment to raise his posterior from the chair in order to vent some slight intestinal pressure. Paaarrrpp . . .—'that was all a cod, on account of the superstitious nature of the man. I had only to tell him I was born in the same city, on the same day as himself, to be quids in. Do you see, he thought we had the same whoroscope, so to speak.'

He laughed unpleasantly at the repetition of this ancient pun of Beckett's.

'But he is dead and you are not,' I said. 'Not yet.'

A long pull of whisky rattled down his throat. He offered me the bottle. I declined it, as he knew I would. I had rather kiss a syphilitic whore than drink from the same bottle as he.

'By God, you are right,' he said. 'I'm not dead, not yet. It was him believed in all that guff, not me. By God, superstition was not in it. A rabbit's foot in every pocket. Speaking of black cats, if you told the poor bastard you'd seen wonna dem in Montmartre that was the last time he would set foot in it.'

'To business,' I said, wishing to leave the place as soon as possible. 'Show me the complete manuscript. If I am satisfied it is genuine and complete, I am authorised to offer you £2,000 for it.' I expected argument, haggling. To my surprise, McFee merely said, 'That'll do. Wait till I get it.'

He produced it, without further ceremony, from under his bed, where it reposed, a thick bundle of paper, tied about with faded blue ribbon, next to a pisspot the contents of which I will not describe.

'Two thousand will do me very well,' McFee said with a sigh. 'Amn't I an old man with both feet in the grave. I'll not have time to spend it.'

I was by the door.

'There will be a cheque for you in the post,' I said. A spasm of agony struck me where the phantom handbag had landed. McFee detected the pain on my face.

'Did you hurt yourself?' he said.

'A bad dream I had,' I said.

'Ah,' McFee said. 'He's come, has he?'

'What?' I said.

'Nothing,' McFee said. 'I said nothing. You know something?'

'What?'

'I was a better writer than he was. Many's the wan that said that, but, do you know, he'd never let me write. He still won't.'

'Rubbish.'

'We'll see,' McFee said, with a valedictory belch. 'I may not be superstitious, but I never said I didn't believe in ghosts. Good luck with the writing.'

I fled.

That night I dreamt that I was beaten up by Ernest Hemingway with James Joyce egging him on. I woke up with a black eye, broken ribs and the near-certainty that I was going mad.

Poindexter, at lunch the following week, was inclined to dismiss the fears I harboured for my sanity. 'It is a well-known fact,' he said, flashing his cuffs over the linen at the Terrazza Est, 'that all writers are stark raving mad. You wouldn't be writers if you weren't. Ipso facto, you cannot be threatened with insanity. You are already insane. Just get on with the book. It will make us both rich.'

'You are already rich,' I said. This was true, by my standards, at least. Poindexter wore £500 worth of Italian tailoring on his back and spent his weekends on his 2,000 acres of Surrey. 'What about McFee?' I said. 'It hasn't made him rich.'

'No need.' A sliver of *osso bucco* passed over expensive dentistry. 'The bugger snuffed it.'

'He what?'

'Snuffed it. Last Friday. They found the body in a dustbin in the alley under his room. A fitting end, you might say. It seems he fell out of the window. Blind drunk, of course.'

I put down my fork from trembling fingers. 'McFee,' I said, 'never opened a window in his life.'

'That's what happens when the poor get their hands on money.' Burgundy washed over the immaculate teeth. 'Changes their life-style, invariably ruinous, even fatal.' Manicured fingernails played on the tablecloth. 'Now this Joyce,' Poindexter continued. 'It is great material, marvellous. I want the book finished by Jan first.'

'I can't do it,' I said.

'If you nip into your bank,' Poindexter said, 'you will find that ten grand has been transferred into your account. That's for starters.'

He ordered coffee and brandy.

It was as he was settling the bill by handing over a strip of embossed plastic that he asked, with an expression of mild distaste, 'Who was your friend?'

'What friend?'

'Baleful-looking chap, sitting right behind you. Saw him glaring at you. You know who I mean, patch over the left eye.'

'Was he, by any chance,' I said, 'wearing a white suit?'

'The same. Friend of yours? I know how you writers hate one another, but . . .'

'I quit,' I said. 'That's it. Finish. You can have your advance back, all of it.'

'All of it?'

'All of it, every farthing. I ask only that my name be in no way associated with the book.'

'Well, if that's what you really want, old boy. But I must say I'm rather disappointed. I shall have to get some hack like . . .'

'Allow me to warn you,' I said, 'that if you are visited in dreams by . . .'

He took no notice of course. There is no restraint to be placed upon the greed of publishers. No matter. It was a splendid funeral. I have been asked to write a biography of Dylan Thomas but have opted instead for the post of Deputy Head of Creative Literature at the University of East Florida.

GRAHAM SWIFT

Myopia

It can't be helped. To be expected. You get older. The symptoms manifest themselves.

That day, for example (a month after my forty-third birthday), when I visited the optician's. My increasing short-sightedness.

Short-sightedness? I wouldn't have known it was that, I wouldn't have called it by that faintly derogatory name—were it not that I noticed that other people waiting in the queue saw the number on the approaching bus long before me; were it not that familiar faces, encountered in the street, would smile and greet me even before I knew they were familiar faces; were it not for my ten year old son, last summer at the seaside, pointing to an oil tanker somewhere on the horizon and my seeing nothing, but looking in the right direction and saying, 'Oh yes—well spotted!' Were it not for Helen's nagging: 'You want to get your eyes tested.'

You see (see?), I thought what I saw—the fuzzy faces, the illegible lettering on signs, the general impression of cloudy, impenetrable distance, was normal.

My optician smiled. 'A common experience. We all see with only one pair of eyes. What those eyes show us we think of as perfectly sufficient. How are we to know we are not seeing all we could? Now, shall we just examine—'

Sitting in my optician's black leather chair while he shines his spot-torch, I feel a moment's rushing panic. Everyone lives in his own sufficient world, his own cocooned vistas. Then the optician steps down from the heavens with his test-chart and his ophthalmoscope: No, this is how things really are.

'Open wide.'

I stretch my eye-lids; give a big optical 'Ah'.

But you see, it wasn't the fuzzy faces or my son's perspicacity, or even Helen's nagging (I could have endured all these) which prompted me into this visit to the eyeman. It was my wife's more than eager attendances at Mr Hogan's keep-fit classes. You see—you see—I started to think I ought to open my eyes in other ways too. To act on what I saw. I said to myself, if I wanted to make sure of this Hogan business, the first thing to do was get a pair of glasses.

'Uhuh,' said my optician, non-committally, retracting his torch. 'Now, shall we try the chart.' And he dimmed the lights in his consulting-room, switched on his fluorescent test-chart and he put a heavy, multi-disced contraption over my eyes.

'Read the letters, please.'

I read the first row, the second, the third. Easy. It was only with the last two rows that I admitted difficulty. But not bad.

Then a disc came down over my left eye.

'Again.'

I read the first line. And the—but, wait a minute, the second line was already playing tricks on me. And the third and the fourth. They were like letters seen through a film of tears. I faltered, went dumb.

Off came the left-hand disc, down came the right-hand one.

'Again.'

'E . . . C . . . F . . . B . . .' Silence. Dismay.

I never knew this. This is cruel. I can't make out even the simplest things. I am being humiliated.

And suddenly my optician ceases to be an optician. He is the remorseless teacher at infants' school, knocking into us the rudiments of reading, pointing to the letters on the board while I (a reluctant learner) avoid his eye.

'Ah . . . Buh . . . Kuh . . . Duh . . .'

Please, teacher, please don't ask me to read.

These keep-fit classes started last autumn. I knew nothing of Hogan then. The Adult Institute prospectus listed courses of morning sessions for women. My wife put down for Tuesdays and Thursdays. I didn't object. I positively approved her initiative. You see, it was an indication that she, too, felt her body was beginning to betray her. She, too, thought she was growing old.

'Fine. Great idea,' I said.

But when I learnt that my wife's instructor on these breathy mid-week mornings was a Mr Hogan—*Mister* Hogan—I became —curious. I had pictured some sinewy games mistress; iron-haired, bugle-voiced. Very well, 'he' was a 'she'. But when I subsequently discovered that this 'he' was not only a 'he' but a 'he' in the mould of Charlton Heston, I began—to be nervous.

I had no qualms until I saw the man. Hogan. It *sounded* too rugged, too muscular for the reality not to be different.

But then, one Saturday in January, as Helen was driving us back from shopping, she spotted Mr Hogan on the pavement. 'Look,' she said and gave a toot on the horn, 'Mr Hogan.' I craned and squinted over the dash-board; but I didn't have to be presbyopic to see that Mr Hogan was built to heroic proportions: that he did not walk so much as loom; did not stand so much as tower; that his face—its features were the usual blur but I could see this much—was one of those strong, firm faces which have a permanent tan, no matter the season or the weather.

We came to a halt in a queue for traffic-lights. Hogan was

opposite us on the far pavement. Helen wound down the driver's window. I couldn't see Helen's expression, because her head was turned; and I couldn't see Hogan's because I am short-sighted. Then Helen turned, gave me a quick, darting glance, looked for an instant into her lap, then through the window again at Hogan. I don't know why, but this little series of movements made me suddenly very anxious to know the look on Hogan's face. I leant across to peer over Helen's shoulder. I screwed up my eyes. But I couldn't see; I couldn't make it out. The lights changed. Helen nudged me back on to my side. And it was then that she said, almost savagely, as we moved off: 'You want to get your eyes tested.'

'Well—' My optician lights up his consulting-room again; takes the visor from my eyes, '—there's no doubt that you need glasses.'

He writes on a card.

'I assume you don't drive, Mr Sharpe?'

'No. Er, my wife does.'

'Well you're way below the standard required.'

He continues writing.

In my black leather chair I venture plaintive inquiry.

'This short-sightedness—is it likely to get worse?'

He looks up. 'How old are you, Mr Sharpe?' (All right, no need to rub it in.) He consults his card. 'Forty-three. No, I doubt it very much. You see, myopia usually begins in the teens.' (So I've always been like it, always not seen the world for what it is.) 'It probably reached its peak in your twenties. You became accustomed to it.' (A condition of life then.) 'I dare say it's got no worse for several years.' He leans back in his chair. 'As a matter of fact—given your age—your eyesight may well improve. You see, as people grow older, their near-sight usually becomes poorer—reading-glasses and so on. That is, they become relatively long-sighted. But if you're short-sighted in the first place, the one effect tends to cancel the other. Your sight becomes better all round.'

I smile wanly at my optician. Suddenly I am beginning to like him.

And then after that encounter with Hogan in the car, I began to think. I began, as they say, to put two and two together. The kids at school; old enough to come home by themselves. Myself at work. The whole of Tuesday and Thursday afternoons clear. Supposing Hogan says—as Helen lingers after the class: 'How about a spot of lunch with me, Mrs Sharpe?' And supposing they have lunch; and supposing one thing leads to another . . . ?

Is this just another symptom of getting old? This growing paranoia. This growing sense of things going on that you can't quite see—things being said that you don't quite catch. Like at work, where I imagine them whispering when I'm out of the room: 'Poor old Sharpe . . . missed the boat . . . be where he is till pension-time . . .' This sense of having blinkers put on you . . .

Was it just concidence that during this period Helen would frequently seem lost in thought, need to be spoken to twice before answering? Just coincidence that when I approached her in bed she would utter the old excuse, 'I'm tired'? Though what she meant was not 'I'm tired' (for she'd been keeping fit) but '*You're* tired'.

Or perhaps she *was* tired. Really worn out. Particularly on Thursday evenings . . .

Hogan. It ought not to be allowed. All those middle-aging housewives, stripped to their leotards.

Do you know what I started to do? I started to use my nose. It's what you do when your eyes don't help. I sniffed my wife; my wife's clothes; our bed; the living-room sofa; the back seat of our car. Sniff, sniff, sniff, like a dog—it's what we all do, shamelessly, when we're eaten up by suspicion. Even the ones with hawk-eyes.

'Yes, Mr Sharpe, your vision could well improve . . . but for the time being, glasses . . .' My optician smiles reassuringly, consults his file-card. 'Your prescription is straightforward. They could be ready in a fortnight. My receptionist will help you choose the frames.'

It's my cue to get up out of the black leather chair. But I pause. I rather like this consulting-room; its confidentiality; its womb-like darkness; the little lit-up puzzleboard of the test-chart.

He lingers out his smile, a trifle impatiently, a trifle quizzically, as if he were saying perhaps: Shall we talk about the real trouble now?

'Was there anything else, Mr Sharpe?'

And suddenly the room changes again. Not into a chalky school-room this time. At the press of an invisible button the black leather chair folds back to form a couch. A row of calf-bound tomes replaces the rack of instruments. Some tranquil, soft-hued painting—a still-life, a landscape—replaces the test-chart. He sits by the couch, chin resting on clasped hands . . .

'So you believe your wife actually . . . with this man Hogan . . . I see, I see . . . do tell me more . . .'

What wonders a bit of glass over the eye can perform. I picked up my glasses two Saturdays later. All that weekend I was like a man after a miracle cure. I went for walks in panavision. I never knew that wintry trees had so many, individual twigs. I never knew that grass was not some green matting but rank upon rank of little vivid spears. Never knew that the silhouettes of rooftops and chimneys against a February dusk could look so delicate . . .

And I never knew how people existed so much in their own outlines—distinct, separate . . .

And these marvellous inventions: glasses. Better still—*spectacles*. How quickly you strike up relations with them. How quickly they become companions, friends-in-need—shields, weapons, comforts. How quickly you learn all the little tricks: looking over them, looking under them; taking them off; waving them in one hand; rubbing them; huffing on them; settling them on the nose . . . Better than cigarettes.

But, no—I didn't forget. These glasses were also a label, a tag, a mark for scorn. The first Monday at the office, I waited for someone to say it: Hello four-eyes. So now you need crutches for your eyes too.

And then Tuesday came. I had planned it all. I took the day off from work, but Helen didn't know. I dressed in my usual work suit; I left the house at the usual time. But I didn't go to the station. I spent the next four, tensely long hours keeping out of the way, killing time—in a café, in the public library. But at twelve-fifteen—when my wife's keep-fit classes end—I was in position—glasses freshly huffed and rubbed, newspaper ready to hide my face—sitting by the window in The Crown, which lies conveniently opposite the Adult Institute.

My wife's class began to emerge. I didn't need to be told. Strangely, unnaturally frisky creatures. Women happy to be schoolgirls again. Lingering garrulously on the pavement. Fifteen or so appeared. Three of them made a bee-line for the pub and came and stood behind me with lagers and limes. No Helen. I sweated. Then one of the swing-doors of the Institute opened; opened and was held open; and out slipped Helen, almost shyly, ducking her head slightly, like an animal being let out of a cage. And whose arm was holding back the door? Whose massive chest was she ducking under? Hogan's. The trio behind me—watching what I was watching—gave a little heckling chorus. I sweated.

Would they cross to the pub too? No. They turned to their right along the pavement, side by side, Hogan carrying a sports bag in his left hand, right arm swinging free. I got up from my seat, my drink half finished, barged through the ladies with their lagers and out on to the street.

They continued walking on the opposite pavement. I shadowed

them on my side, keeping just behind them. Lines of parked cars by each kerb provided a sort of screen. Perhaps my new glasses made me invisible. After about thirty yards, Hogan reached in his pocket and produced a key ring. What detail! What clarity! They stopped by a car—a low-slung, zippy little machine that looked too squat for Hogan to get into. Hogan walked round to the driver's side; unlocked the door. As he threw his sports bag on to the back seat and eased himself in, his face was momentarily lifted and turned half towards me. My new optics revealed no flaws in that indelibly tanned face. No weak mouth, no flabby jowl. Oh Mr Hogan was Mr Perfect, all right, Mr For-ever-in-his-Prime.

I thought: now he will open the door for Helen. But he didn't. Helen bent down by the passenger's window. A brief exchange. Hogan waved, clipping on a seat belt. So it wasn't a lie. I'd asked Helen if she drove to her classes. She said, no, she walked—only right, to a keep-fit class. I'd thought: Aha—Hogan provides the transport.

Hogan pulled out into the road. Helen remained on the pavement behind a little cloud of exhaust vapour. She didn't wave. But she didn't move from where she stood, even when Hogan's car had disappeared. I stood behind a parked van, watching intently. Come on glasses, tell me, tell me.

She stood still, she didn't move. Then she plunged her hands suddenly deep into her coat pockets and made a little swivelling movement without moving her feet—the way little girls sometimes do.

And then I *did* see.

Helen wasn't carrying on with Hogan. She had no claims on this giant of a man. But what Helen did have was a little Platonic crush. She had this thing about Hogan, as some thirteen year old schoolgirl has about a lean-limbed maths teacher. It really *was* like being back at school. My thirty-eight year old wife was happy being a child.

I watched her through my new glasses. I was touched, touched.

To think I had planned revenge. She stood there on the pavement, alone, distinct. We all live in our own world. I slipped away down a side street . . .

And how did I spend the rest of this furtive, vigilant day? Lunch, in another crowded pub. People's ultra-sharp faces. Walking in the park, exercising my new vision. A February afternoon. The colours of pigeons' breasts matching the tones of the sky. Little chill drops of water rolling off ducks' backs . . . At three-thirty I gave up loitering and went to meet my children from school.

A hubbub at the school gates. Without my glasses I might never have seen them.

But I spotted them. Kathy, David. Two individuals.

'Daddy, what are you doing here?'

'Oh, I came home early from work. Thought I'd meet you.'

Kathy is evidently pleasantly surprised. She smiles. I think Kathy likes me in glasses. Her smile somehow makes my day. David is sullen and holds his distance. He doesn't approve of this sudden intrusion on his independence. He can get home fine by himself.

As we walk, Kathy takes my hand and looks up with a little shrewd adult face, as if she's already learnt the art of seizing the right moment to ask delicate questions.

'Daddy—Mummy goes somewhere on Tuesdays, doesn't she? And on Thursdays too. Where does she go?'

'You mean that you don't—' And I'm amazed that Helen has never told them, has never wanted to share with them this experience of needing to go to school again, of needing a teacher —a PT instructor, an optician.

'Oh, she goes to keep-fit classes—at a school for grown-ups.'

'What's "keep-fit", Daddy?'

'It's—it's something you think about when you're getting old.'

We are standing on the pavement, forced to wait for David,

who is dawdling skulkingly behind, not wanting to catch up.

Kathy frowns. 'Daddy, why do we grow old?'

I look at my daughter. I think of what changes, what traumas lie in store for her, only a few years ahead. And then I realise that in the hackneyed fashion of those about to impart wisdom (as though to put a mist between myself and Kathy, myself and the world), I have taken off my glasses.

I can't answer her question.

GILES GORDON

Madame Durand

I rang the bell.

Someone had to, if it was to sound, if a response was desired.

I wanted a response, hence my ringing the bell. Hence the 'I', the first person.

I stood outside the house, in the street, waiting. Cap in hand? No. Cap on head? No. It was a hot day but no cap, no hat. I stood in front of the closed door.

Was it locked, and if so from the inside or the outside? There was no way I could tell without turning the door handle, trying to turn the handle. I didn't want to make a fool of myself, or appear to be an intruder, an unwelcome visitor. What if I had turned the handle, the door declined to open and someone had observed my action? What if I had turned the handle and the door had not been locked but my hand had proved insufficiently strong to open the door?

I rang the bell. Waited.

'Durand,' read the name plate screwed into the door frame immediately below the bell. 'M et Mme Jacques Durand.'

I was in France. Durand is a common name there. Very common. Like Smith or Brown here. Perhaps Jacques Durand is a less common name than Jean Durand.

I was in the country, a small town.

Behind me, traffic. Peugeots, Citroens, Renaults and others. French cars, of divers manufacture, plus a smattering of foreign plates: GB, B, D, I, NL and others, though more rarely, less frequently others, an A and an L, I remember, and others. The vehicles pulled and wheezed, trundled and shot up the hill, the narrow road behind me, leading towards the centre of the old town.

My back was to the traffic, my face to the closed door. I rang the bell.

Below me, out of sight from where I stood but still below me, the Cher glided its sinuous way towards or away from the Loire. I couldn't tell which direction without recourse to a map. My map was with my belongings, and they were not with me.

I rang the bell, finger on the bell, off it, had rung it, stood there, facing the door. I stood there, feeling self-conscious. My hair out of place? I don't think so. No, not self-conscious, that's wrong. Feeling nothing, not knowing who (if anyone) would appear, whether Madame Durand, or Monsieur, or another. A little Durand, perhaps; or a domestic, if one was employed by the Durands. It was hard to gauge from the façade, the front door of the detached house, detached but with houses nestling against it on both sides, how well off the Durands were, their status. The name plate, for instance, presented no clue. It didn't proclaim that Monsieur Durand was, for example, a doctor or lawyer, a butcher or baker.

In the crypt of the XIth century church, so notices and posters indicated, wine was being served. Wine, I ask you. In a medieval church. But France is France and if you can't drink wine—hold a wine tasting—in a church, why should it be possible to drink it elsewhere, in a bar or at home, outside or inside?

The day was hot. Hot? It was sweltering. Mid-August. French families that hadn't gone abroad, or had no intention of doing so whether for financial or cultural reasons, or simply tradition, were playing in public parks or bathing or—in the case of many adults—sunbathing or pedalling boats on the Cher or the Loire or the Seine. Children, mostly in tow with elegant mothers, bathed and splashed and played ball or board games. Fathers, having sired the next generation, spread out on the banks of the rivers, in braces, having devoured the Camembert or *petit suisse* or wine or maybe all three, not to mention sausage and bread and fruit. The sun smote their faces, their red or brown faces, and they didn't realise or understand that they were being smitten.

I rang the bell. I say: I rang the bell. I remember.

She (why should I have assumed it to be a woman? Do women usually answer the front door bell? Are women more likely than men to be at home during the working day?) took her time in coming. If she was at home, in the house. If she was coming. Child, domestic, Madame Durand.

The bakers of the town, I assure you, were out of baguettes. Sold out of baguettes by 5.00 pm? That was unheard of. French bakers are never sold out of baguettes. Yet the bread is always fresh and often, in the mornings, warm.

The wine, in the *alimentation*, was cheaper—at its cheapest, the *vin de table*—than most other produce, including milk. What, F2.35? There were no more new potatoes. The mushrooms were huge and velvety, like marshmallows or H-bomb clouds. They smelt of the earth, a writhing, rotting conspiracy beneath the surface.

The fruit was luscious.

The sun smashed down on stone. Lizards wriggled and zig-zagged as if they felt they had to, were in danger. Risks were being run.

I rang the bell, pressed the button.

There was, in the town, pervading the atmosphere, a smell of coffee, and of Gitanes (but where was the blue-grey drift of smoke?), and, especially, a whiff of drains.

A gun was fired. Twice. Hunters? Or a car that backfired? Twice.

The door was opened.

A face, female. Madame Durand? Clearly.

'Madame Durand?' I said, leaving a first name out of it, her first name; had I known.

She smiled. 'Oui,' she said, somehow expanding the single syllable, the three vowels into two syllables, two words almost. 'Oui.'

She said it once. Once.

'Madame Durand?'

'Oui,' she said. I thought at first that she said it as a statement, but it was a question, an upward tilt, an inflection. Not that she didn't recognise or acknowledge herself, that she was Madame Durand, but that I was enquiring after her, confronting her. We were face to face with only the open doorway between us, and she did not recognise me, remember me.

'Madame Durand?'

'Oui?'

'Je . . .' I said, began. Then, as her smile continued (parallel lines never meet) but had a question mark behind it, I changed tack. I had to.

'Pardon,' I said. The smile, her smile for I was not smiling, began to fade, like a flower that lives for a day's breath only, for one day. 'Pardon, madame.'

For it was not her, she was not she.

I knew, knew at once.

'Pardon, madame.'

'Monsieur.'

She spoke so politely, as the French do in such circumstances. What circumstances? She understood nothing of what was going on, nothing. I repeated my apology, my explanation.

'Pardon, madame.'

She said again, repeated: 'Monsieur,' then the door began to close, the smile to wither. Indeed, it began to dissolve quickly, only her past—her entire life to that moment—her upbringing and the society in which she moved, directed that the vestiges of the smile remained, in shadow until the door was closed and I was blotted from view, ceased to be three-dimensional. The fact there was glass in the upper panels of the door was immaterial as it was opaque, green too. It served neither as a means for Madame (or Monsieur) Durand to see from within who was without, desirous of intruding or at least make a request of either or both of them, who was standing in front of their front door, having rung the bell; or for the person or persons without to see within. Nor did it serve as a glass for the visitor, keen to be assured that his or her hair, his or her face was in place before the door was opened from within and the Durands' world, the world that was the Durands', joined his or hers, or positively resisted doing so.

'Madame Durand?'

'Oui.'

'Pardon . . .'

I turned round, a movement of legs and body and head. I turned round, insofar as it was necessary or appropriate to turn, and began to walk away before the door was completely shut, became one with the front wall of the house, after Madame Durand had displayed no sign of identifying me, no recognition.

'Madame Durand?'

'Oui?'

Had I seen her before, had we known each other—not just my knowing her—however that phrase be construed? How could I remember? The search, the search for what she was had become interminable. She triggered nothing off in me, no particular response.

'Madame Durand?'

'*Oui!*'

Had she expected someone, a friend, neighbour, someone to mend something, a tradesman, her husband even, even her husband, but would Monsieur Durand have rung the bell unless he was playing games with Madame Durand, or had forgotten or mislaid or lost his key or had left it in the pocket of a pair of trousers which he wasn't wearing? In which case, had she known, expected him and wondered when she answered the ring of the front door bell if I was he, if she could—in the few seconds I stood there—penetrate my disguise and see therein her husband, Monsieur Durand, her Monsieur Durand, her Jacques, Jacques

himself? Had she done so, had she thought that I was he (whether
I was or wasn't, you understand), would she have drawn me into
the house, even into my own house, offered me a drink, embraced
me, gone further, seduced me . . . as if, as if . . . she hadn't seen
me for many a day, didn't recognise or remember me as her
husband but as a lover? But then would she have embraced me at
all, seduced me?

I have said nothing of her age, her attractiveness or otherwise.
They are not the point. They are an irrelevancy, a distraction.
Besides, all such matters are subjective, even a woman's age. She
was a woman, Madame Durand was.

'Madame Durand?

'OUI?'

My direct question, my uttering of her name to her face, forced
her to reply, to provide either a yes or a no. A non-committal
answer would hardly have done.

'Madame Durand?' 'Non.' And a look of surprise that I could
have mistaken her for another, even another Madame Durand.
But she didn't say that, didn't deny the name of her husband, the
fact that she was married and to Durand and that this was her
house as much as it was his, or at least that she lived there. Her
name was by the bell, on the plate. I was in search of Madame
Durand and had found her, found one of that name, therefore
denial would have been useless. No citizen is free from simple
questioning by another, although it is not obligatory to answer.

'Madame Durand?'

'Oui.'

It was I who denied her, I who, after investigating the relationship, withdrew from it. Briefly? Life is brief, depending upon
how you approach it, depending upon your perspective.

'Pardon,' I said. And madame. 'Pardon, madame,' and she
knew, she realised that it was not for me even if it was or might
have been for her, even if it was her husband or lover or would-be
lover walking away from his life with her, their life or lives
together, leaving her, leaving her for always.

'Monsieur,' she said, not uttering my name, not giving anything away.

'Pardon,' I said. 'Pardon, madame.' And turned as it was
necessary for me to do to continue or resume my progress up the
street, the hill towards the centre of the town, the old town.
According to Michelin the church, with or without wine tasting,
was interesting; and there might be an antique shop or two as
well as sign posts to Blois, Orléans, Châteauroux, Tours.

'Monsieur,' she said, and made to close the door, our lives
separated. Was it a question, or a statement, a courteous farewell,
even a request to remain?

'Monsieur.'

Her life and mine had no more in common, we were divorced.

I walked in the strong light, the seething heat, up the parched
hill. Cars, motorcycles and the occasional lorry honked and
thundered, lurched and squealed and bounced up the one-way
road. I read the mass of signposts clustered near each other.
Piscine—Plage, Blois 38. Contres 17. Bléré 32. Base Plein Air.
Stade. Centre Ville. Autres Directions. La Maison du Vin.
Camping. Gendarmerie. Hôtel du Moulin. Grand Hôtel. Vierzon.
In a few days time—at Blois, or Bléré, or Contres—I wouldn't
remember Madame Jacques Durand, that particular Madame
Jacques Durand. Between now and then there would be many
more—'Madame Durand?' 'Oui'—as in the past there had been.
Everything always seemed to happen in the past, especially things
that did happen.

St Aignan-sur-Cher? Charming little town. Once visited it.
Durand? Jacques. Monsieur and Madame? I shook my head.
Don't know anyone of that name. Not the sort of name you
forget, Durand. You don't forget Jacques Durand, Monsieur and
Madame Jacques Durand. Didn't know anyone at St Aignan. A
holiday, yes. Passing through when visiting the châteaux of the
Loire. Personally, I find Chenonceau the most delightful. It's easy
to imagine those romantic meetings in the gardens, behind hedges
and across drawbridges, in corners and secret rooms, behind

screens. What's that? Diane de Poitiers? Can't say I ever did. What *wouldn't* I have given to have known her!

JACK TREVOR STORY

The Investment

'Frank went to Brighton,' said Jill. 'That's what he used to do.'

'I was so fed up,' said her best friend Alice, who had decided to get married and stay in England and not go out to Africa, to Botswana or wherever it was. The Voluntary Service Overseas had smashed the Bromley disco where life had appeared to be one long dance among an endless pattern of available heads all strobed and manifest for her delight. She had married one of them and immediately got pregnant. With the light on, however, she had discovered that she did not love him.

'We don't love each other at all,' Jill said.

'I don't know how you can live with somebody you don't love. I couldn't live with somebody I didn't love. Ugh. I couldn't let him even touch me. Jill, it's immoral to sleep with somebody if you're not in love with them.'

'In the bush it isn't. In the bush you sleep together just to keep warm.'

'Jill, I think that's awful! I never liked the bush. They're all the same up there. That's why I never went. Well, after that one time.'

'Not Shepherds Bush! I mean in Africa. We broke down all the time. How would you like to spend the night in a jeep surrounded by wild animals. Frank killed a hyena. Africa made him a different person. He used to keep going down to Brighton and picking up married women. I mean he was really a sexist pig before he joined the VSO.'

'It wasn't like that with Tony,' Alice said, thankfully. Jill was back and Alice had at last got somebody she could confess to. What happened on that mad weekend in Brighton was the greatest secret of her life. Nobody would believe it, except, perhaps, Jill. The reason was that it was entirely spiritual and not many people knew about spiritual things. In fact, now it came to it, Alice was beginning to wonder what Africa had done to Jill. They were sitting together in one of the less touristy parts of Westminster Abbey—which had seemed to Alice an appropriate place—but somehow Jill was spoiling it. Africa had not only changed her, it had made her brown. Alice's mother had always considered Jill to be ladylike and discreet and now here she was talking almost like a man.

'You don't know how awful people are when you're pregnant,' Alice said. 'The men treat you like some kind of animal and the women keep knitting things for you. You saw me at three months, didn't you? Yes, you did. That was when I came to see you off at Heathrow. Well honest to God, I was out here by October. Everything sticking out like a sack of coal and all at the front.'

'Thin girls always show it worst. You ought to see the blacks at the mission. Talk about a thimble on a matchstick. Look at that girl talking to the Archbishop of Canterbury. She must be nine months at least.'

'Is that the Archbishop of Canterbury? I thought that was in Kent.'

'I daren't go a yard from my doorstep if I was like that. I'd be afraid of dropping it in the street. Here, Alice, can't we go somewhere we don't have to keep whispering?'

'I was nine months when I ran away to Brighton. Everybody said it was going to be a boy. Everybody said stop smoking, stop drinking, do this, do that. People prodding you. I mean they can't wait to get at it, can they, pinch its little cheeks. You feel just like a container. One of those containers. I couldn't get into any clothes. I was wearing old night-dresses in the end. Keeping my knickers up with Sellotape. I'm sure God didn't make women

to have babies. Something must have gone wrong. Then Donald
brought that bloody girl home. You know, Zuleika. Used to do
the limbo? She's at Marks and Spencers now. Skinny as a rake,
no chest. He loves that. He thinks they're boys, I think. Of
course they had to dance, didn't they. He hadn't touched me for
three months.'

'That's ridiculous that is, Alice! You can go with each other
right up to the time almost. There's different ways of doing it—'.

'Oh, don't you start, for Christ sake! That's another thing, you
see. Everybody finding positions for you. There's no privacy left.
Uncle Mac came round when everybody was out. He wanted me
to lay flat on my back on the floor and keep the bottom of my
spine flat with my knees up. You know he's always on about
yoga. That's just an excuse, really. He just wants to get hold of
you.'

'Who's Uncle Mac?'

'Your dad!'

'Oh! Is that what you call him? I didn't know that. Mum'd go
spare! He used to be a—what's that when you manipulate people's
bones?'

'Filthy old beast. Oh, don't worry, he's not the only one. Some
men really get a kick out of pregnant women. It's the one time
you can't pretend you don't do it. Do you know what I mean?
Even my own uncles. Even my brother-in-law. Telling me all the
things he did for Greta. My God, I had to get away, Jill. I just
packed up and waited for Donald to come home—I mean I didn't
want the police after me or anybody dragging the river. I said I'm
off to Brighton for the weekend. You can't do that he said. You're
due on Wednesday. I don't give a sod about that I said. I've
found a train and I've booked a hotel and I don't want anybody
coming down there. What you going to do all the weekend by
yourself in Brighton? he said. I said I'm going to drink and
smoke and have lovely meals and watch the waves. He said you
must be mad. You notice he didn't say who with? Jealous swines
if there's a chance of a girl getting a bit of stray but not once

you're a bloody big fat animal with an old night-dress stretched over your navel.'

'What happened?' asked Jill.

'Look at that bird! Is that a pigeon? Fancy getting pigeons in Westminster Abbey! The Queen got married here, didn't she? It's funny to see all these tourists. Like a bloody shop. Those American girls are all teeth. You watch that one with that old man in a kilt.'

'That's her mother! It's the sun that does it. Africa was like that. You keep calling women sir. How did you meet Tony, then? I mean if you were like that?'

'I hate Americans. I'd rather live in a fog than go around barking on one note. Tony was different, you see, that's the whole point. This is what I'm trying to tell you. Do you know what I mean? He didn't even notice I was pregnant! I swear to God he didn't notice!'

'What did Zuleika want, then?'

'Oh, you know. More bloody woollies. I mean they roll in it, don't they? Soon as anybody's in the club. All their sodding abortions come flooding back. I hadn't seen her for a year. I don't know whether Donald has, mind you. She was keen on him, wasn't she. Well, you told me that. Otherwise I wouldn't have looked at him twice.'.

'Don't blame me, Alice.'

'I'm not blaming you, Jill.'

'Donald was a good dancer.'

'I know that. That's not what it's all about is it, dancing? The silicon chip society. You should have seen them that night she came round. Letting his shoulders go loose and nodding his head like a bleeding Muppet. That's about ten years out of date. Oh my God, Jill, it brought it all back. Straight out of school and down the disco.'

'That's exactly what Frank says! That is precisely what Frank said to me in Botswana. Dancing and drinking and drugging and screwing—'

'Jill! For heaven's sake remember where you are.'

'That's why he kept going down to Brighton. Until the earth-quake in Turkey—five thousand people killed. Sleeping out of doors in the freezing cold, whole families. Do you remember? One of his married women put him on to Volunteer Service Overseas. That's where her husband was. She was pregnant.'

'Surely she didn't go with him while she was pregnant?'

'Oh no. Frank is very cool indeed, Alice. I want you to meet him. You would never think he was cool at first. I know I didn't. He laughs at lot.'

'Tony laughs. He's got a lovely smile. This is it.'

'Frank seemed to open out after he'd killed the hyena. He fancies himself as the great white hunter. He reads a lot. Books.'

'Tony reads books.'

'That's good, Alice.'

'There was some in the hotel reception. I stayed at the The Grand—'

'Frank stayed at The Grand—he used to work there rather.'

'He didn't! That's where Tony was. In the Grotto bar.'

'Frank was on keys. They probably know each other.'

'I don't think so, Jill. I hope you don't mind me saying this. Frank doesn't sound like the kind of person who would—well, get on with Tony. Killing animals and picking up married women. I doubt whether Tony ever picked up a woman in his life.'

'Oh, come on, Alice. You're so hypocritical. He picked you up, didn't he? You said so. Well, don't look like that. Isn't that what you've been telling me?'

'No it damn well isn't, Jill. It wasn't like that at all. Tony fell in love with me and I fell in love with him—that's all. Nothing physical took place. Perhaps you wouldn't understand that, coming out of the jungle. I've met some Franks. I know all about Franks—'

'Don't shout then. People are looking. I think there's a christening. It's a marvellous place, isn't it. Look round and be talking about the architecture.'

Jill and Alice mastered a very faint and pious smile for a reconnoitering verger. Jill managed to hum *As I Survey The Wondrous Cross* now being played by the organ. Alice whispered quite fiercely, 'I wouldn't bring you to Westminster Abbey to tell you about a dirty weekend in Brighton.'

'I'm sorry. Truly.'

'Well, this is it,' said Alice.

They listened to the rest of the hymn and watched some well-dressed people around the distant font.

'It was fantastic, Jill. He only had eyes for me. I mean there was a lot of competition. Friday night, just before dinner and not just residents. There was some smashing birds there. I mean they made me feel like a bloody hippopotamus. I'm not kidding, Jill, he could have took his pick. Even the ones that was escorted couldn't get unstuck from the bar. Every time Tony served anybody he kept coming back to me, d'you see. I was up the end of the bar by the plants. Well, I thought I might get mistaken for a cactus!' She screamed like a diesel and both forgot their surroundings for a moment. On the disco circuit around Pénge, Crystal Palace, south westers, they had shone like two pretty stars, Jill the quiet one, cocooned brunette favouring little dark symphonies of colour, Alice always frilly at the edges but conventional in the middle.

'Having a big belly wouldn't stop your sex appeal,' said Jill. 'Just a bit of promise if you ask me.'

'What do you mean by that?'

'What's he like, this Tony, then? Mum didn't mention any Tony. She just said you'd gone to live with your mum and dad and taken the kid.'

'What do you mean by a bit of promise, then? Is this your Frank talking, then? Because don't confuse that kind of dirty thinking with Anthony Billingdon. I mean I could have been a man, Jill. Do you understand that?'

'What's Donald going to do now you've left him?'

'I tell you what we had, me and Tony. Instant something—rapport. He told me how they make Campari. Things like that. His mother died when he was four and he was brought up by a aunt who had thirty cats! She used to give Tony saucers of milk. I hope that chap's not coming over here. Pick up that prayer book. Look at those lovely windows all different colours. It's like what's that you have to keep shaking?'

'Kaleidoscope. It's all right, he's gone. Have you been here before? Howja know where to come? I would never dare come in here by myself. The times I've passed it. People in Botswana don't understand that. This chap in the slaughterhouse wanted to know all about the Tower of London. Old Frank laughed his head off—oh gawd, here we go, I mustn't start giggling. No, he said the tower is probably the crème de la crème for slaughterers all over the world.'

'Laughed his head off!'

'No, don't start for gawd's sake or you'll set me off. Think of something serious. Has Donald got access to the child?'

'No bloody fear.'

'What happened then?'

'I wouldn't trust him near Nathan.'

'What do you mean, Alice?'

There were three distinct organ chords and then a silence and Westminster Abbey seemed to have altered its centre of gravity towards the girls from Bromley, Kent.

'He tried to murder me, that's what.' Friends since Bromley infants, the two girls struck the same inner communion of horror, face to face in the Abbey pew, as the time when two dogs coupled in the playground.

'Donald did?'

'I woke up with a pillow on my face.'

'Oh, my God, Alice!'

'Three times!'

'Alice! I can't believe it! How could you go to sleep any more?

I'd have sat up all night.'

'You know Donald has asthma? You know that's why he had
to give up dancing? You know he has to have three pillows at
night? You know how when he turns over he's always poking
me in the eye with his elbow? That time I had to wear an eye
patch just when Miss Bromley was coming up?'

'You weren't married then!'

'We were engaged if you don't mind, Jill Tweedling.'

'I'm sorry. I didn't mean that. I was just remembering that eye
patch—d'you remember other girls started wearing them? They
thought you were being trendy. The war in Israel was on then
and there was that prime minister or general or something. No,
go on—oh look at that baby!'

'I don't want to look at any bloody babies.'

'What do they do actually? They just wet its head, don't they?
Baptists duck you right under—here, I wonder if they lose any?
There's a lot of people going out. They're not waiting to close,
are they?'

'You know how nylon pillow cases slip off? Well I used to go
to sleep on my back and gradually—I was lower than him—his
pillow would come across right over my face. No listen, this is it
really, one night I couldn't knock it back! He was laying right
on top of it! It was awful. I couldn't get my breath or anything.
Oh Christ. It was terrible. You try it. Cover your face up—no,
don't take a deep breath. This is it. You wake up with empty
lungs—oh Christ I shouldn't do that, it brings it all back.'

'Whatever did you do, Alice?'

'You see my fingers? You hold them stiff and pointed together
like a tent—like a dagger really. Then you dig 'em hard up under
his ribs—no, not there, just there, harder—'

'Oh! God almighty!'

'I know! That's your spleen. It's better than a fist if you get the
right point, it goes right in. People go unconscious and sometimes die. If you do it too hard you can split the spleen. The police
have to learn that—you remember Charlie? It's one of the law

and order exercises. Anyway, it woke Donald up I can tell you. Talk about levitation!'

'You should have gone to the police.'

'Charlie said they have to be present while he's actually doing it. I mean that's bloody silly. At first I thought he was genuinely asleep but when I saw him banging heads with Zuleika that night I thought to meself, well, you know. If I leave him or he leaves me he has to give me half the house money but if I peg out all she has to do is move in. I think they're starting evensong. I brought mum here one night after we lost the dog and they were singing evensong.'

'So what happened in Brighton, Alice?'

'Oh, Jill, it was beautiful. All he did was shake hands with me when I came away on the Sunday. I think that was the only time he touched me. On the Friday evening I just saw him in the bar while he was working and that was all. Do you know what, just being with him and all those other people about, he made me forget that I was nine months gone. He was shy and he liked my hair and told me about his past. Tony comes from East Ham. He worked at Becton Gas Works till they made him redundant but he wouldn't go on the dole. He answered an advertisement for a trainee chef at the Black Diamond on Kingston by-pass and switched to bar work when they were looking for cocktail and aperitif learners and something a bit better. That was only a few years ago yet he's got three thousand pounds in a building society already and he's going to buy a house whether he gets married or not. As an investment.'

'That's what it was,' said Jill. And then at her best friend's sharp attention she closed her mouth, firmly. Alice knew this expression of old. 'What what was, dear?'

'I think we ought to go. They're lighting candles.'

'What what was, dear?'

'If you're going to get upset at everything I say.'

'What what was, Jill?'

Jill gave an immense sigh and her eyes roved the cathedral for

help. She said: 'You're not going to hit me with your handbag?'
Alice said, calmly, with the knowledge of her recent spiritual
experience, 'I'm not even angry with you, Jill.' Jill said: 'Right.
You know when I said that having a big belly wouldn't stop your
sex appeal? Well I really meant that, sincerely. I'm sure you felt
like a slag but you never look like one. You're a dainty person.'

'Oh, boy!' Alice nodded her pretty head round an invisible
audience. 'I remember the last time you said something like that.
Okay, my head's on the block. Bring it down. Let's get it over.
Here's my handbag, you hold it.'

'I'm sure I don't know what you mean, Alice.'

'What do you mean by my big belly being just a bit of promise?'

'Oh, that.'

'Yes, that, my little snide friend.'

'There's no call for that. I'm talking about Frank, not Tony.
It was his word for pregnant women. Neglected women. Women
fed up like you were, running away to Brighton. Oh, you're not
unusual, Alice.'

'What was his word?'

'Investment,' said Jill. 'Not promise.'